''You can't feel guilty. We didn't do anything.''

At that Hedy cast Ty a guarded look. ''But we spent the night together.''

''You really are an innocent, aren't you?'' He shook his head. ''This doesn't mean we're engaged, you know. I have the classic bachelor's attitude toward marriage. I'd rather be thrown to raving sharks.''

Her cheeks burned, and she knew she was blushing. ''Who said anything about marriage?''

''I did,'' he replied easily. ''I said it terrifies me. I mean, I should tell you that up front, right?''

''Why should I care what you think about marriage?'' she asked coolly.

Ty savored a bite of biscuit. ''A woman should always care what a man thinks about marriage—if they are going to be involved.''

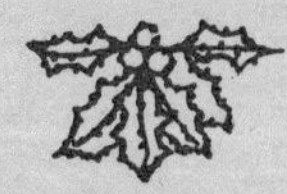

Dear Reader:

We hope our December Harlequin Romances bring you many hours of enjoyment this holiday season.

1989 was an exciting year. We published our 3000th Harlequin Romance! And we introduced a new cover design—which we hope you like.

We're wrapping up the year with a terrific selection of satisfying stories, written by your favorite authors, as well as by some very talented newcomers we're introducing to the series. As always, we've got settings guaranteed to take you places—from the English Cotswolds, to New Zealand, to Holland, to some hometown settings in the United States.

So when you need a break from the hustle and bustle of preparing for the holidays, sit back and relax with our heartwarming stories. Stories with laughter . . . a few tears . . . and lots of heart.

And later, when you get a chance, drop us a line with your thoughts and ideas about how we can try to make your enjoyment of Harlequin Romances even better in the years to come.

From our house to yours, Happy Holidays! And may this special season bring you a lasting gift of joy and happiness.

The Editors
Harlequin Romance
225 Duncan Mill Road
Don Mills, Ontario, Canada
M3B 3K9

THE SNOW GARDEN

Bethany Campbell

Harlequin Books

TORONTO • NEW YORK • LONDON
AMSTERDAM • PARIS • SYDNEY • HAMBURG
STOCKHOLM • ATHENS • TOKYO • MILAN

ISBN 0-373-03019-3

Harlequin Romance first edition December 1989

To Les and Martha From

Printed in U.S.A.

CHAPTER ONE

SHE WAS ALONE IN THE HOUSE for the first time. The rooms held an almost eerie silence, as if waiting for something to happen. She tried to ignore the house's air of sadness, its feel of being ever-so-slightly haunted.

Stepping to the tall windows of the front room, she parted the tattered curtains. The brief Illinois autumn blazed early this September. Red and gold leaves already littered the grass of the lawn.

A green and white sign stood at the yard's edge. In bold letters it announced SOLD. In smaller characters it proudly stated, Another Happy Home Owner—Thanks to Casper Realty Company!

And I'm the happy home owner, Hedy thought in wonder.

The Sold sign gleamed in the sunlight because of her, Hedy Hansen. It didn't seem possible. She felt the house might suddenly dissolve like a dream and she would awaken back in Michigan, in the bedroom of the old farmhouse where she had grown up.

No. Michigan was behind her now. The farm belonged to someone else. It was part of the past, something to be forgotten. She had escaped as her mother had wanted her to. This was the fresh start, the new life, in a beautiful suburb of Chicago. In her own house.

Hedy turned from the windows. The problem was that she didn't yet feel as if the house belonged to her. It still bore all too clearly the imprint of its former owner, Mr. W. A. Tidwell, deceased. *Invader,* the house seemed to say to Hedy. *Stranger. Intruder.*

She shook her head. She was being too imaginative. The house was hers. She had bought it as soon as she'd sold the farm in Michigan. Her cousin Jolene, who owned the Casper Realty Company, and on the side purchased old houses, renovating and reselling them, had recommended this house to Hedy as an investment and sold it to her.

Jolene was not only the family beauty, she was the family success story, as well. Twelve years ago she had left Fox Creek for the bright lights of Chicago. Now she was not merely well-to-do; she was, by anyone's standards, fabulously wealthy, a woman who had made her way.

For years Hedy had fantasized about following in Jolene's footsteps, at least a little way. She hoped to make a modest living restoring houses, work she knew she could love.

When she was certain the farm in Michigan was going to sell, she had presumed to call Jolene. Breathless with excitement, hoping she wasn't imposing too much on her important cousin, Hedy had asked her to help find the house that she had dreamed of.

She knew exactly what she wanted: a structurally sound house, suffering only from neglect, located in a desirable suburb of Chicago. A house that needed only imagination, elbow grease, and tender loving care to increase its value dramatically. A house that would bring bountiful rewards to the person willing to work hard enough for them.

Miraculously, Jolene had had exactly such a house listed.

She had insisted Hedy act swiftly before someone else snatched it up. "Don't even bother to come see it—don't risk the time," Jolene had advised. "Trust me. Grab it." Hedy had done exactly that.

But now, standing in the dusty living room, Hedy experienced a sinking feeling. The old house was more neglected than she had imagined. The wallpaper hung in tattered strips, the carpet was stained and threadbare, cobwebs festooned every corner.

And in spite of Chicago's famous winters, there was no central heat. Instead, a gigantic and frightening-looking gas heater was attached to the dining-room wall. Jolene, who should know, assured her it would heat the whole house. Hedy hadn't wanted to contradict her, but she didn't see how it could.

The furniture, which had been sold with the house, didn't cheer Hedy much, either, although Jolene insisted it was a bargain of nearly mind-boggling proportions. Everything was old, out of style, and scarred with use.

The one truly lovely piece in the room was a large mirror with an elaborate gold frame. The images it returned were cloudy, for its glass needed resilvering, but it had the potential of being lovely—with work.

Work, Hedy thought, lifting her chin, she needed to get to work, that's all. She wasn't afraid of work; she had spent all twenty years of her life on a farm that greedily devoured labor. Only here, in Chicago, she would have something to show for it—unlike her parents. The tree farm had killed them, it was as simple as that. It had worked them to death, first her father, then her mother.

But she was young and strong and she was going to take charge of her life. She had worked out a master plan and she intended to follow it. Nothing—and no one—would stop her.

She looked at herself in the clouded mirror. It reflected a tall young woman who looked both determined and a little frightened. Her body was slim but firm, and she was still tanned from summer. The Michigan sun had streaked her brown hair with gold and left a sheen of rosy bronze on her high cheekbones.

Her mouth, full and prettily curved, would have looked vulnerable if she hadn't kept it strictly controlled. Her real beauty lay in her eyes; they were the deep blue of hyacinths, wide, expressive, and long-lashed.

Her eyes marked her as her father's daughter. He, too, had had such eyes, improbably beautiful for a man. Every time she looked into a mirror, she remembered him, dead of a heart attack when she was fourteen, his lovely eyes closed forever. He and Hedy's mother had been very much in love, and theirs was a home full of laughter. When he died, Hedy missed him terribly, and what she missed most was his laughter, his sense that although life was difficult, it was an adventure, too, full of small and surprising joys.

Hedy and her mother had tried to run the farm alone. Instead the farm ran them. It took over their lives, claimed their every waking moment. Hedy's mother, Katherine, had tried to keep her sense of humor, and somehow, by joking about their troubles, they were able to survive them. But only for a while.

Last winter, right after the tree harvest, Katherine Hansen had had a stroke. She was still a young woman, but she had simply worn herself out. Her concern was not for herself, but for Hedy, and it became almost an obsession.

She told Hedy to put the farm up for sale. "Leave Fox Creek," her mother had said, "go to Detroit or Chicago or Grand Rapids."

It had been wrong to keep Hedy tied to the farm, her mother kept saying. It was wrong for them to have stayed so stubbornly in Fox Creek, where few chances flourished for the young. She should follow Jolene's example and make something of herself.

Never get attached to a place, her mother had warned her; learn to let go of things. Use your head, not your emotions. Pursue something and do it seriously. Go where the opportunity is, Katherine Hansen kept repeating. She had a second stroke at Christmas. She did not survive.

Memories of her parents made Hedy's eyes sting with unshed tears. Blinking them back, she looked away from the gold-framed mirror. She was still in some kind of shock, she knew, and she wondered if she would ever be quite the same again. Alone, in a strange place, she felt dislocated, disoriented and numb. But she was, at last, face to face with opportunity.

She forced herself to be optimistic. The old house, in spite of its years of neglect, still had some beautiful features, like the lovely stained-glass window on the west side of the living room. The afternoon sun glowed through it, jewellike, throwing richly hued patches of light on the worn carpet.

It wasn't much, but it was a cheering start: a handsome mirror and a beautiful window: the house's two genuine and indisputable treasures. They would give her the courage to keep going.

At that moment a baseball came crashing through the stained-glass window, then smashed like a bullet into the center of the mirror. As the mirror shattered, the ball took a hard hop on the floor and hit Hedy smartly in the kneecap. It bounced again, then rolled to a stop.

She stood, openmouthed with horror. The beautiful window lay in an explosion of multicolored glass and the remains of the mirror glittered like a hundred little daggers. Her knee throbbed so hard that tears once more smarted her eyes. For a moment she was too stunned to be angry.

Then she snatched up the baseball and strode to the front door. She tried to push it open. She didn't know what child had done this, but his parents would hear about it, she thought grimly.

But the door wouldn't open because someone was pushing from the other side. She seemed to be having a door-pushing contest with an invisible opponent, and it only frustrated her more.

"Stop pushing!" ordered a disgusted masculine voice. "The door pulls open—from your side."

Hedy, startled, quit pushing. She stood glaring at the door as it swung open easily. A man stood there. A very tall man.

He was wearing cutoff jeans, a Chicago Cubs T-shirt, and the most disreputable-looking sneakers she had ever seen. He stepped into her house as if he owned it.

He looked down at Hedy. He smiled a self-effacing smile, raised his eyebrows in a skeptical shrug and reached out, taking the ball from her hand. He tossed it casually into the air and caught it neatly. "Thanks," he said. "Sorry."

Hedy looked up at him in amazement. The man radiated a good-natured insolence, a light-hearted irreverence. "Sorry?" Her disbelieving blue gaze almost made the air crackle. There he stood in her living room, staring at her boldly, as if he had more right to be there than she did. "Is that all you're going to say—*Sorry*?"

He moved one shoulder in a gesture of helpless boredom. He tossed the ball again. "It seemed like the right word. *Le mot juste.* How about 'very sorry?' "

He studied the righteous resentment coloring her cheeks. "Okay," he tried again. "How about 'I'm slimed with shame?' Do you have any sackcloth and ashes? I'll wear them in penance. Would that satisfy you?"

"No," Hedy shot back, completely unnerved. "Paying for the damage would satisfy me. And who are you, walking into my house like this? Who hit that ball? If it was one of your children, he should know better than to hit a ball toward somebody's house."

He surveyed the piles of broken glass on the floor. "Hmm," he mused with scientific interest. "Two with one blow. I never did that before. Not bad."

"*You* hit that ball?" she demanded. He nodded with satisfaction. She put her hands on her hips and scrutinized him.

At first glance he seemed all height, lean muscle and wavy, brown hair. She estimated that he was thirty or so. Not that he dressed it, or for that matter acted it. He had the air of a man who would still seem young at eighty.

He had a runner's body, with disconcertingly long legs, no hips, a washboard-flat stomach, a deep chest and well-knit shoulders. He was as tanned as if he did nothing but lie in the sun all day, and his tousled hair was darker than hers. His brows were darker still, thick and curving slightly. His chin had an impudent cleft.

There was really nothing remarkable about his face at all, Hedy decided, except for the sheer derisiveness that shone out of his eyes. The eyes themselves were neither green nor brown, but some indefinable color in between.

He surprised her with a smile that was almost shy. "Hey," he drawled, "I'm sorry. Really. This is a lousy way to meet. You're the new neighbor, right?"

So, thought Hedy nervously, his nonchalance hadn't worked and now he was going to try charm, was he? He was radiating quite a lot of charm, he was good at it, but she intended to let him know it didn't affect her in the least. Hedy Hansen was made of sterner stuff.

"You really hit that ball?" she repeated. "I can't believe a grown man would be so irresponsible—"

"I hit it," he admitted. He gave her a look that indicated she should have been more impressed. "My nephew was pitching. He threw an illegal spitter that came at me like a guided missile. I tried to kill it before it killed me. A clear case of self-defense. My name is Ty Marek, by the way."

He had his thumbs hooked into the front pockets of his cutoffs and stood, his weight on one foot, his head cocked confidently. He tried another smile, this one of a more devastating caliber. "And you're too pretty to fight with. I think I love you."

"I don't want you to love me," Hedy returned, disconcerted. "I want you to pay me."

The curved brows raised in feigned shock. "You can be bought? This is better than I'd hoped. This is a bachelor's dream. I'll go home and get my piggy bank."

"I most certainly *can't* be bought," she protested. He seemed determined not to take the situation seriously, but she was equally determined to force him to do so. "This room had two decent features—the window and the mirror—and you broke them both before I'd been in the house an hour. You also hit me in the knee."

He followed her gaze downward. She wore a short denim skirt, and they both could see the round bruise forming on her knee.

"Offhand," he muttered, "I'd say your *knees* were the two most decent features in the room. They're heartbreakingly cute. I think I love your knees, too. I'm sorry about the bruise—sincerely."

"Just pay me for the window and the mirror," she said, her patience seriously overloaded.

His frankly appreciative stare made her even more ill at ease. The man didn't have an ounce of decency in him. She crossed her arms instinctively in self-protection.

"Ouch!" she said involuntarily. Drawing her hand away from her sleeve, she looked down at her fingers. They were spotted with blood. She was cut—and her blouse probably ruined.

"I don't believe this," she said in disgust. "I'm surprised I wasn't killed by flying glass."

"Don't be melodramatic," he commanded. Before she knew what he was doing, his hands were on her, turning her so that he could examine the cut at the back of her elbow.

She flinched at his touch, but there was something mysteriously compelling in the sureness of his movements.

"Aha," he mused. "The culprit." He drew a small shard of amber glass from her sleeve. "Sorry again. Your blouse is cut, too. But you're not bleeding too badly."

"That's easy for you to say," she remonstrated, pulling her arm away. "It's not your blood."

"True." He smiled kindly, but the light in the green-brown eyes was mocking. "Maybe we should take off your blouse. Just to check the cut. I've had extensive first-aid training. Honest."

"I'll leave it on," she said, uttering every word with dangerous distinctness. "Now you owe me for a blouse, too, Mr.—Malik."

"Marek," he corrected. "You never told me your name. Is it Venus? Is it Aphrodite? Perhaps it's simply Beauty."

"It's Hedy Hansen," she retorted, trying in vain to see the damage inflicted on her blouse and her arm. "That's Hedy with a 'y' and Hansen with an 'e'. So you can spell it right on the check. This blouse was brand-new. The mirror needed work, but that window was in perfect shape. And it was an antique. I don't know how I'll ever replace it."

"I do," he said, grinning easily. "I've replaced it six or seven times. I'm an expert on replacing that window. And it's not a priceless antique. It's exactly a year old. Really, Hedy, stop twisting. Roll up your sleeve and let me look at your arm."

"You mean you've broken this window *before*?" she asked in dismay. The man was an irresponsible maniac. Worse, he was her own personal next-door irresponsible maniac. But without knowing why, she rolled up the sleeve of her white silk blouse—formerly, her one truly good blouse—and let him examine the cut. His hands were surprisingly gentle.

"I've made a career out of breaking that window," he said. The sunlight falling through the broken window gilded him.

"Always with a baseball?" she asked with forced pleasantness.

"No. That would be boring. Once with a croquet ball and once with a golf ball. And once with a jar of pickles."

"A jar of pickles?" she cried. "How on earth—"

"Don't ask," he ordered. "It's not a pretty story. Come into the bathroom. Let's wash this off and put a Band-Aid on it." His hand was warm clasping her arm, and he steered her unerringly toward the ancient bathroom.

She went without protest, conscious of how tall and absolutely sure he seemed of himself. She was distracted because he somehow seemed to smell like autumn, of breezes, leaf smoke and sunshine. She was also perplexed about the jar of pickles, but he was probably right—she was better off not knowing the story.

He opened the medicine cabinet and began sorting through its contents. Once more she thought it politic to squirm away from him, but he held her fast. The little bathroom seemed too cramped and intimate for two people, especially when one was as tall and full of controlled masculine energy as Ty Marek.

He hummed under his breath as he set a bottle of antiseptic, a bag of cotton balls, and a box of Band-Aids on the edge of the sink.

"You know your way around here awfully well," she said suspiciously. "How come?"

"W.A. was a good neighbor," he said simply. "An extraordinary man. But he's gone. I'll have to make do with you, I guess."

He swabbed her arm expertly and applied a bandage. "You're welcome," he said, although she hadn't said thank you.

She rubbed her arm gingerly. She found herself staring up into his face, wondering again just what color she would call those disturbing, laughing eyes. The half smile on his mouth seemed just as much a riddle.

"Welcome to the neighborhood," he said. She licked her lips nervously. He watched the movement of her tongue carefully, as if he were memorizing it.

Hedy squared her shoulders, embarrassed, and marched past him, rolling down the sleeve of her ruined blouse and rebuttoning it. She had more important things on her agenda than making inexplicably charged eye contact with an irreverent neighbor. He had no place in her master plan; hence, her life.

He followed her into the kitchen, his hands in the back pockets of his cutoffs. He was humming again as he watched her rummage in the kitchen closet until she found a worn broom and a rusted dustpan.

He looked at the cobwebs hanging from the ceiling corners, the scarred cabinets, the scuffed tiles of the floor. "You're brave to take on this place," he observed. He straightened a crooked drawer that had lost its handle. "It's a mess."

Hedy, insulted, glanced at him, a brief shot of blue fire. "It's a bigger mess since you entered the picture. Here. You can sweep up the glass." She thrust the broom and dustpan into his reluctant hands.

"Whoa!" he exclaimed. "Do you ever say anything polite—like please?"

"Clean up the mess you made—please."

He shrugged. "Since you beg." He sauntered toward the living room and Hedy stalked behind him like a guard with an untrustworthy prisoner.

He bent, the muscles in his long thighs rippling, and started to sweep the broken stained glass into the dustpan.

"You never said where you were from," he challenged. "You don't sound like Chicago."

"Michigan," Hedy answered shortly.

"Detroit?"

"No. The closest town's too small for you to know."

"Try me." He dumped a load of glass into an old metal wastebasket and began sweeping up another.

"Fox Creek." She folded her arms again. The very name of the town filled her with sadness and a nameless anxiety.

"I've heard of Fox Creek," he said, surprising her. "I remember hearing of it—vaguely." His tone no longer sounded playful, but almost bitter. He swept silently for a moment, then emptied a second pan of glass and began on the third. Whatever his shortcomings, he was a demon sweeper.

"You said that was the closest town." He squinted up at her through a wayward lock of wavy hair. "You from a farm?"

She turned away, staring out the front windows. "Yes."

"Yeah?" he asked, his former good humor returning. "I always wanted to live on a farm. Cows and horses and pigs."

She hesitated a moment. Her bruised knee throbbed, her cut arm stung, but a deeper hurt eclipsed the pain. "We didn't have animals," she murmured. "It was a Christmas-tree farm."

"Sounds great," he said. "Like something out of a kids' book. You'll fit right in. We make a big deal out of Christmas here."

She turned to face him, her chin set staunchly. "I *hated* that farm." The suppressed passion in her voice made him blink. He stared at her, reappraising her.

She wanted to bite her lip, but kept her expression blank. What she had told him was true. The farm had killed her parents. It had dominated her life for years. It had filled her mother's last days with guilt and regret. Hedy never wanted to see another Christmas tree as long as she lived.

His expression grew more guarded, as if he suddenly didn't like what he saw.

"What do you mean, they make a big deal of Christmas around here?" she asked, trying to sound casual.

He finished sweeping up the largest of the mirror fragments. "This street. Holly Street. It's kind of famous. Everybody decorates for the holidays in a big way. W.A. started the trend. If you bought his furniture, you've probably got his Christmas decorations—an attic full. This house was always a real showplace."

"Well, it won't be this year. I—I don't have time for that kind of silliness."

"It's a tradition," he said quietly. He had risen to his feet, and again she was conscious of his height.

"Traditions can be broken," she said tartly. "Give me that broom."

"Gladly," he said, yielding both it and the dustpan into her hands. "Maybe you can ride it back to Michigan."

She gave him an icy look. He had hurt her feelings, but she wouldn't give him the satisfaction of knowing. "Jolene didn't tell me anything about Christmas," she muttered. She went back to the closet to put the cleaning implements away.

He followed, lounging in the doorway. "Jolene? Jolene her own royal self sold you this house? She probably didn't tell you a lot of things," he said wryly. "I know how she works."

She cast him a disapproving look. "Jolene happens to be my cousin. I'll thank you not to talk about her that way."

"I see." He nodded with an air of a man acknowledging an unpleasant discovery. "Cousins. I should have known. The same hometown. The same blue eyes. The same cold streak. But Jolene at least has the hypocrisy to pretend to be nice."

"I beg your pardon?" she snapped, even more stunned and angered. She shut the closet door and glared at him.

"No," he answered, folding his arms implacably across his chest. "I beg your pardon. I mistook you for a human woman, not a member of the tribe of Jolene, the Ice Queen of the Frozen North. No wonder you never smile. Too busy figuring out ways to get ahead, I bet."

He glanced around the dilapidated kitchen. "You didn't buy this house for a home. You bought it as an investment, right? Heart like a calculator, I'd guess, always computing away."

"There's nothing wrong with investments," Hedy rejoined, defensive.

Ty laughed. "Maybe. Maybe not. But this is rich. Jolene actually unloaded this collapsing old heap on a relative? There'll be investments, all right. And you'll make 'em all. Till it hurts. Wow. Jolene. I never asked if there were any more at home like her. Two of you. Scary. Brr. Break out the antifreeze."

Hedy put her hands on her hips and took a step toward him. She paused in a patch of sunlight that brought out the honeyed highlights of her hair. He looked at her with cool interest but no longer with friendliness.

"First," she said, her voice quivering, "you smash my window and break my mirror. You nearly cripple me with your baseball, you ruin my blouse and spill my blood. Then you insult me *and* my cousin. If there's anything seriously wrong with this house, I know what it is—it's next door to *you*."

He smiled, shrugged, and turned to walk back into the living room. "Funny," he muttered. "That's what Jolene said." He glanced at the floor. "You'll need a vacuum to get up the last of that glass. I don't think I'll do it. You make me feel—how can I put this?—unwanted. I have batting practice."

He strolled to the front door and paused by a plastic case with a wire front and air holes in its top. "What's this?" he asked, his voice faintly insolent, as if he had a right to know.

"My cat," Hedy replied coldly. "She's still tranquilized from the drive."

He gave her a measuring look. "A cat? A pet? Something warm and living? Maybe I misjudged you."

"It's a very expensive Persian cat," Hedy retorted. "I bought her to breed."

He raised his brows in distaste. "It figures. Even sex for profit." He picked up his baseball from the old coffee table where he had set it. He tossed it experimentally. "Cats shouldn't be bred. It's too cold-blooded. They should fall in love or lust or whatever, like everybody else."

Hedy trained a disapproving look on the baseball. "If you're going to keep batting that thing, don't aim it this way. And rest assured, I'll send a bill for the damage."

"Somehow I knew you would," he said with a superior smirk. This time when his gaze traveled over her it was blatantly provocative. "You're a pretty woman," he drawled. "Wound tight as a watch spring, but pretty. That's some consolation. Ciao, lady. Happy house repairs."

He reached down and patted the animal carrier in which the cat still lay groggily. "Good luck, cat. You'll need it."

He opened the door, and the late-afternoon sunshine flooded in. "Uncle Ty!" came an adolescent wail. "It's about time! Did you find a girl in there?"

Ty tossed Hedy a parting glance over his shoulder. "My nephew. He of illegal-spitball fame." He opened the door, calling to the unseen boy as he did so, "Stay cool, Tadzio. It's a girl, but she's no fun. Come on. I'll pitch."

He left, long legs striding easily across the lawn, a slight swagger in his walk. The sun gleamed on the unruly brown waves of his hair. "Tadzio! Catch!" he called, throwing the ball swiftly and with impressive strength.

She looked after him a moment, her heart beating hard with resentment. Then she shut the door. No fun, was she? Who would be after encountering him—and his nearly lethal baseball? Damned overbearing, presumptuous, and self-satisfied man. Irresponsible and smart-alecky, too. What a way to start restoring the house, by losing both its best features in the space of a second. *What a welcome to the neighborhood,* she thought.

But now that the man was gone, the place seemed unnaturally quiet. Arrogant as he was, he radiated vitality as strongly as the bright autumn sun radiated light. There had been something oddly appealing in his refusal to be serious, something that reminded her of happier times. But he hadn't seemed to like her one bit.

She shook her head. She realized, guiltily, that she hadn't been on her best behavior, either. But he had caught her in a lonely and anxious mood, and he had rattled her badly.

Bits of glass still glistened on the carpet, too small for the broom. She would have to vacuum, and she supposed W.A. Tidwell, deceased, had a vacuum cleaner tucked away somewhere, if she could only find it.

She paused for a moment to peer into the cat cage. The cat, a gorgeous Persian with a perpetually brainless expression, looked out at her with glazed, golden eyes.

His remarks about the cat had hurt particularly. It was true she'd bought the animal as an investment—she hadn't even bothered to name it.

But she liked the idea of having a pet. Her motives weren't simply materialistic. She was as human as anybody, no matter what the scathing Mr. Marek said. She wondered, puzzled, how he knew Jolene and why he seemed to dislike her so much.

He had even implied Jolene would take advantage of Hedy, which was ridiculous. For years, Hedy, like other girls in the family, had idolized Jolene. Hedy wanted only to follow her example, to be a woman in charge of her own destiny, secure and safe.

She shook her head again, trying to dispel the memory of Ty Marek.

"Hello, Kitty," she said halfheartedly to the cat. Perhaps she should start working on their relationship now.

But the cat only stared through the bars, looking as if it had a massive feline hangover. It refused to engage in meaningful communication.

Work, Hedy reminded herself. If she was going to get her life in order, she might as well begin.

She changed into her jeans and an old shirt. She started working in the kitchen, cleaning cupboards, countertops, and scrubbing the floor. She labored late into the night, until she was too tired to worry about anything, least of all her presumptuous neighbor.

The cat, now fully conscious again, complained softly. Hedy fixed its litter box, set out its food and water, and let it out. She sat on the sofa and watched as the cat warily explored, its plumy tail waving apprehensively.

A born aristocrat, the cat did not seem happy with its new surroundings. Hedy, bone-weary, looked about the room and did not feel overwhelmed with enthusiasm herself.

In the dim light the room seemed smaller, drearier, more careworn. There was no longer the beauty of the mirror or the stained-glass window to console her. Instead there was only a tarnished, empty frame—and a gaping, dark hole in her wall, through which a chill breeze stirred.

She tried talking soothing nonsense to the cat, as if it were an ordinary barn cat back in Michigan. The cat simply stared at her, as if insulted.

Hedy sighed, snubbed. The cat didn't want to be friendly, but maybe it would help if she named it. That would create at least an illusion of chumminess between the two.

She didn't think of a name for the animal until she fell into bed, too tired even to undress. Then, lying there in the darkness of the unfamiliar room, she knew what she was going to call that strange, empty-headed cat who was now her only companion.

Despite her fatigue, she smiled. She would name the cat Security. Hedy's mother had hoped that her daughter would one day have security. The cat would be a living symbol of that hope.

Hedy would have fallen asleep with Security tight in her arms if the cat had allowed it. But instead, as Hedy drifted into sleep, the cat wandered the house, complaining nervously, as if something were terribly wrong.

Its cries haunted the dark house.

CHAPTER TWO

WHEN HEDY AWOKE in the morning, Security had vanished. Although she searched the house from the attic to the most obscure nooks of the cellar, she could find no trace of the cat.

Hedy stood in the living room, disoriented and close to tears. She ached from working late into the night, but the house looked every bit as dingy as it had yesterday.

And now beautiful, golden-eyed Security, who had cost three hundred dollars, was missing.

Worse, although Hedy didn't know where the cat had gone, she knew *how* it had gone. The only way out was through the broken window. Hedy had been too tired last night to think of the window as an exit. Under her breath, she once again cursed her heedless neighbor.

She would have to go out and search block after block, hoping the cat hadn't gotten itself permanently lost or been hurt or taken. Looking for the cat—when there was so much else to be done.

She plodded fatalistically to the bathroom and started to brush the tangles from her sleep-tousled hair. She changed her jeans and sweatshirt for clean ones.

Who knew how far she'd go before she found that beautiful idiot of a cat—if she could find it at all? Chicago was big enough to hold six million people—or was it eight million—how would she ever find one wayward cat?

Just as she finished knotting her shoelaces an impatient knock rattled the front door. Perhaps it was the man from the phone company, she thought in consternation, come to connect her telephone. He'd delay her search for the cat even longer.

She pulled open the door, her despair mounting. Ty Marek stood on her porch, wearing dark blue running shorts, a blue handkerchief bandana twisted into a headband, and no shirt. His chest was deeply tanned and covered with curly, dark hair. Hedy started in embarrassment at the unexpected sight of so much masculinity towering on her doorstep.

His mouth crooked at one corner. "Could this," he asked, holding up a large, fluffy ball of gray, "be yours?"

The cat blinked its big yellow eyes at Hedy, as if it were thinking of something infinitely far away. It seemed content to hang inertly from Ty Marek's hand.

"Security!" Hedy cried happily, throwing open the screen door.

"What?" said Ty Marek, frowning.

"You found her," Hedy exclaimed with relief. "Oh, Security! You scared me to death."

"What?" repeated Ty. "Security? What?" He looked down at her suspiciously as she took the cat from his arms.

Hedy scooped the cat to her breast and hugged her. "My cat. She ran off. Where'd you find her?"

"In my garden," he said somewhat acidly. "Assaulting my pumpkin vines. A man who's just had his pumpkins attacked should at least be offered a cup of coffee. How about it?"

Hedy, still hugging the cat, froze. She looked up at him, her blue eyes darkening with apprehension. "I haven't made any coffee."

"Then I'll make it," he said, again stepping into her house as if it were his own. "I need caffeine, only as a reward for not turning that furball into compost. What's wrong with her, anyway? She acts like she's never been outside before."

"She hasn't," Hedy said, hurrying after him, still carrying the cat. "I just bought her. She's spent most of her life in a pen."

"That's criminal," he snorted. "Where's your coffeemaker?"

"I haven't got one," she replied in frustrated confusion. "If you want coffee, it'll have to be instant."

"That's criminal, too," he said grumpily. "Oh, well, it's my greatest culinary skill, anyway—boiling water."

He switched on the burner beneath the kettle, then turned to face her, leaning his rangy body against the counter. "You'd better keep that cat in," he warned, "until she learns to be a real cat. A cat that's never been outside—" he ended with a sound of disgust.

Hedy scowled at the tall, half-naked man lolling in her kitchen. "She got out through the window *you* broke," she accused.

"Don't blame me," he muttered, lifting one tanned shoulder in a careless shrug. "You're an adult. You should have covered the window."

In perplexity, she pushed one hand through her thick brown hair. The man was maddening, an insolent and irresponsible intruder. Worse, his long legs and bare chest somehow distracted her, making her pulse hammer and her face feel hot. She took a deep breath to calm herself. He had an effect on her she didn't understand, and it made her angry.

"I didn't ask to be lectured," she stated. "If you don't like the way I do things, leave. Go finish your—your jogging or whatever." She tossed her head and tried not to notice the way the morning sunshine gleamed on his shoulders.

"I don't jog," he answered sarcastically. "I don't run, either. I've made a sacred pledge to myself never to travel farther than five blocks by foot—and never faster than at a stroll. I've dedicated my life to ease."

"Then why are you dressed like that?" she demanded.

He looked down as if he'd forgotten he was dressed at all. "Oh." He gave her a conspiratorial smile. "I like to saunter over to the park and pretend I've been jogging. That's all."

"Pretend to jog? What for?"

He looked in her cupboard for mugs and coffee and found them immediately. "So I can look at the Canarsi twins." He adjusted his headband to a more rakish angle. "The Canarsi twins *really* jog. In these tight Spandex suits. A legend in their time, the Canarsi twins. Also, Myra Rubikoff is usually out running. Excellent muscle tone, Myra."

Hedy narrowed her eyes. "You pretend to jog so you can watch women? That's lecherous."

"Yes. And pleasurable," he answered without concern. His expression grew pensive. "But I've missed them today. Because of your, you'll excuse the expression, cat. You'd better watch her. I won't be responsible if she gets out again."

He turned his back to her. She stared at the subtle play of his muscles as he spooned out the instant coffee and poured the water. His arrogance was truly colossal. "I doubt if you've ever felt responsible for anything in your life," she snapped. "And I don't know why you'd claim responsibility for my cat, anyway—she's no concern of yours."

He turned back to face her, a mug of coffee in each hand. He set them on the kitchen table. He favored her with that agitating smile of amused superiority. "Sex," he said simply. "Have some?"

"What?" Hedy demanded in disbelief. She took a step backward.

"Have some coffee?" he said, sitting down. "As for sex, I mean the cat. Have you looked out your back door? Do. You'll see what I mean."

Puzzled, Hedy went to the back door and stared out. At first she saw nothing out of the ordinary, but then she saw *it*. For a mind-numbing second, all she could think of to call the sinister object was "it."

"What's that—*thing*?" she asked in horror.

It was cat-sized, but not cat-colored. It was muddy brown with dark, tigerish stripes. It seemed to have no ears, and its pale gray eyes, glittering maliciously, were slightly crossed. She had lived in the country all her life and had never seen such a beast. Perhaps it was some sort of gigantic mutant, earless, city rat.

"That," Ty said proudly, "is Benchley. My cat. A *real* cat." He raised his mug and took a sip of coffee as if toasting Benchley.

"That's no cat. It hasn't got ears."

"He lost them. Benchley's led a life of adventure. Don't you want your coffee?"

She tore her eyes away from the hideous creature crouching on her back porch and moved to the table. She did need coffee, she needed it badly. She picked up the mug and stared down at Ty suspiciously.

"How did your cat lose its ears?" She took a long, bracing drink of the black brew.

He leaned his elbow on the table, looking pensive. "He disappeared one winter. He accidentally got locked in the Golds' garage when they went to Hawaii. His ears froze. Gives him sort of a streamlined look."

"It gives him a demonic look." She shuddered. "Why is he that color? Why are his eyes like that?"

Ty's green-brown gaze raked over her as if he were insulted. "He's a crossbreed. Part Siamese, part alley cat. But he's all cat—which is more than I can say for that fluffball you're holding. So watch her. She was prancing around in the pumpkin patch for his benefit."

Hedy set down her half-finished coffee with a thump. "My cat would never *prance* in front of yours."

"Wouldn't she?" He waggled his eyebrows wickedly. "You didn't see her—I did. It was passion in the pumpkins—no doubt. Keep her in. Or, like I say, I won't be responsible. Benchley's seduced cats all over this suburb. The virile devil."

Hedy stared daggers at Ty Marek, who seemed invulnerable to them. "If your cat so much as lays his weird eyes on Security again—" she began.

"I'm not responsible," he finished, standing up and putting his mug in the sink.

"I mean it," she said, trying to sound convincing. His height was truly impressive and it disconcerted her to have to look up so far at someone.

"I mean it, too," he replied, rinsing out his cup. "I believe in nature. When better cats are bred, passion will breed them, not parsimony, not pecuniary interest, not pelf."

"What?" Hedy demanded again, bewildered.

"Not money," he said, turning toward her and taking a step in her direction. "Attraction is more important than money. It's more important than anything. It is, as they say, what makes the world go round."

He moved nearer still. She didn't understand the look in his eyes. She only knew that his gaze, the color of antique bronze, made her heart race at a stammering beat and caused strange prickles to travel through her blood. She looked down in embarrassment and found herself staring at the curling brown hair on his chest.

In confusion, she looked back up into his face. It was a mistake. His smile seemed to have some hidden meaning.

Again she was assailed by the autumnal scent that seemed to emanate from him, as if he carried his own aura of sunshine, wood smoke, and tangy breezes.

"Lord, your eyes are blue," he mused. "Blue as the long, prairie twilight. I once loved a girl with eyes that blue."

His gaze flicked to her lips, then back to her eyes again.

Hedy felt she was completely losing her balance. It was as if she were falling, against all laws of gravity, *up* into his eyes.

His smile became gentler, more intimate. "No," he corrected himself huskily. "I think your eyes are even bluer. I'd kiss you—but you'd take it wrong."

"What do you mean?" she asked, amazed at his audacity.

"You might think I like you," he answered, his smile suddenly turning to mockery again. "Thanks for the coffee. And watch your cat. Benchley's no respecter of pedigrees. He's not a respecter of anything. Be careful—or you'll end up with a batch of kittens not worth a dime."

Indignant, Hedy glared at him. He put his hand to his headband in a parody of a salute, then started toward her front door.

She followed, clutching Security more tightly than ever. "I don't want worthless kittens," she told him, piqued. "You keep that, that monstrosity away from us."

"Benchley goes where he likes," Ty said contemptuously. "I don't control him. Nobody controls him. He's a force of nature, and he's free. If anybody around here keeps a cat prisoner, it's going to be you."

He opened the door and saluted her again. "I really would kiss you," he told her. "If you weren't so uptight. It might be almost as much fun as watching the Canarsi twins in those Spandex running outfits. *Adieu.*"

"Goodbye!" she returned with an uncharacteristic show of passion. *And good riddance,* she thought. He was as awful as his cat.

She slammed the door, then stalked to the bathroom and locked Security inside until she could cover the broken window.

Disgusting man, she thought furiously. *Outrageous, overbearing, arrogant, presumptuous, disrespectful, derisive, smirking gadfly of a man.*

He might be tall and dark and tanned and handsome in that offbeat, offhand, off-center way, but he was as unpleasant as a hard blow to the head. In fact, every time Hedy saw him, that was precisely how she felt, as if she'd sustained a dizzying smack to the skull—slightly breathless and unable to think straight.

She found she was dwelling on what an unpleasant man Ty Marek was and it gave her a perverse sort of pleasure. She amused herself by listing his shortcomings while she taped a large piece of cardboard over the broken window. She enumerated more of his faults while she took down the ancient curtains, washed the downstairs windows, and scrubbed the living-room woodwork.

BY THAT AFTERNOON, fueled by her anger, she had accomplished an enormous amount of cleaning. She had also convinced herself that everything about Ty Marek was unlikeable. He was too tall, too lean, and his hair was too wavy. His eyebrows were too thick, his eyes too exotic, his chest too hairy. He was even too tanned—he must do nothing all day except lie in the sun like a torpid lizard.

Shortly before three, she heard a car pull into her drive. The tattoo of spike heels rang out on the front porch. The doorbell chimed, and almost simultaneously the door was pushed open and Jolene breezed in. She had promised to bring Hedy an extra set of keys early that morning, but she was late. Hedy didn't mind—she had been far too preoccupied counting Ty Marek's flaws.

"Hi," she greeted Jolene. She smiled ruefully and wiped a cobweb from her hair, tried to brush some of the dust from her jeans. Jolene, perfectly groomed, always made Hedy feel like an unsophisticated bumpkin from the unsophisticated hinterlands.

Jolene wore a beautifully cut suit of pale blue suede. Her high-heeled dark blue suede boots matched her purse. Sapphires sparkled in her ears and on her fingers. They were souvenirs of Jolene's first husband, the one who had left her the Casper Real Estate Company. Her present husband, Melvin, always gave her diamonds or pearls.

Jolene was twelve years older than Hedy. Her eyes were the same startling blue, but they seemed unshadowed by worry about money or the future or anything else. Her hair, once the same brown as Hedy's, was now an elegant ash blond. Hedy was frequently told she looked like Jolene when Jolene was younger, but she could never believe it.

Jolene winced slightly at Hedy's jeans and sweatshirt, but gave her cousin a gingerly little hug, careful not to get too close. "Look at you!" Jolene said effusively. "Aren't you as snug as a bug in a rug! This house is *perfect* for you!"

She straightened her suede jacket and adjusted one brilliant earring. Her long-lashed eyes glanced around the living room. She immediately noticed the shattered mirror and the cardboard covering the broken window. "Good Lord, what happened?"

"I met the neighbor," Hedy replied unhappily. "But first I met his baseball."

"Ty Marek?" Jolene dropped her purse on the coffee table and sat down on the worn sofa, crossing her expensively booted legs.

Hedy nodded without enthusiasm.

"Listen. Watch out for *him*." Jolene brushed an imaginary spot of dust from her lapel. "Ty Marek," she mused, shaking her blond curls. "He'll give you trouble just to spite me. Ignore him."

"Trouble?" Hedy asked, disturbed. "To spite you? Why?"

Jolene looked at Hedy, her eyes wide and innocent. "I went with him. In college. He was crazy about me. He never got over it."

Hedy looked at her cousin in surprise. Ty Marek didn't seem like the type to take anything, especially a woman, seriously. "What do you mean?"

Jolene examined her rings. She tilted her head philosophically. "He wanted me to marry him. Instead, I married Larry Casper. When he died, I married Melvin. I'd forgotten about Ty. But when I got this house to sell and we ran into each other again—well, he made it clear he hadn't forgotten me. If he tries to bother you, ignore him. Since I broke up with him, he consoles himself by chasing anything in a skirt. He'd probably love to hurt you—just to get at me."

Hedy looked at her tiny and elegant cousin. "Hurt me, to get at you?"

Jolene shrugged, looking kittenish. "I mean it, little cousin. Fox Creek doesn't prepare you for this kind of man."

Hedy pondered this statement. Ty Marek was certainly irreverent, probably a rakehell, and definitely unlike anyone she had ever met. "He—he doesn't seem to take anything seriously," she said.

"He's probably afraid to—after what happened between us." Jolene smiled mysteriously. "Besides, he can't *afford* to take anything seriously."

Hedy was puzzled. "Why not?"

Jolene blinked her large blue eyes as if surprised by Hedy's naïveté. "He makes an extremely nice living by not taking things seriously. He writes the satire and humor column for the *Trib*. He's syndicated in two or three hundred papers."

"He's T. Z. Marek? The columnist?" Hedy cried. "I've heard of him! I've read him! He's—he's got a bunch of books out."

"Five," Jolene said, looking as satisfied as if she'd written them herself.

Hedy looked up at the mirror Ty had broken. *Ty*—so he was T. Z. Marek, the one and only. Back in Fox Creek she had always checked out every new book by T. Z. Marek as soon as it reached the library shelves. No matter how grim things had been in Fox Creek, T. Z. Marek could make her smile. But his nonconformity, his wild streak, so engaging in print, were another matter, and a disturbing one, in person.

"He really *is* as independent as he acts, then," Hedy said in awe. "I mean, nothing's sacred to T. Z. Marek. He doesn't give a hoot what anybody thinks."

"So he likes to pretend," Jolene answered knowingly. "But I'll tell you again—watch out. He gobbles up little girls like you for breakfast—and stays hungry."

Hedy didn't have to be told she was unprepared for someone of T. Z. Marek's stature. She was as unworldly as the humblest prairie flower and knew it. What sophisticated man would look at her twice? And why would she want Ty to look at her, anyway? She'd spent all day telling herself how much she disliked him.

Still, she was jolted by the news that he had once loved Jolene. Jolted, but, she told herself, it made sense.

Everyone in the family knew that Jolene attracted men the way a particularly sumptuous blossom attracts bees. When Jolene left Fox Creek, she had broken hearts all over the county. Who wouldn't fall in love with Jolene? Everything about her was perfect.

Hedy suddenly felt conscious of all her own shortcomings, her inexperience. She felt like the country mouse of the fable, an extremely threatened country mouse.

"Jolene," she said hesitantly, "Ty—the Marek man—said people celebrate Christmas in a big way on this street. You didn't tell me. I don't think I'm up to it. Will the neighbors resent me if I don't go along with it?"

Jolene's placid expression didn't change. "What do you care? Do what you want. It's a free country. Look, sweetie, you wanted a house that was a steal. I found if for you. For heaven's sake, don't complain. And don't be sentimental about Christmas. All that's behind you now. You've got to grow up. You're a big girl now."

"I'm sorry," Hedy mumbled, feeling rude and ungrateful. She had no right to complain after all Jolene's help.

Jolene gave her a tolerant smile. She stood and picked up her handbag, opened it and dropped Hedy's spare keys onto the coffee table with a clatter.

Jolene shook her head, sighing helplessly. "Just watch out for *him*," she warned, nodding in the direction of Ty's house. "This is a marvelous house. It's got heaps of potential. I'd have kept it for myself if it weren't for him. He still chases me—after all these years. You've got sense. Use it. He'll try to play your feelings like a harp, if I know Ty. Just to prove he can."

Hedy nodded mutely. Jolene's advice was an eerie echo of her mother's: use your head, not your emotions. Her emotions were dangerous, in turmoil from too much grief and change. She must keep them under the tightest rein.

She walked Jolene onto the front porch. Jolene reached out and patted her cheek, smiling the dazzling smile for which she was justly famous. "Listen, I have to run. Melvin isn't well and he likes his babydoll home early. And I want to get out of this warm leather and into a cold martini."

Jolene paused on the top step and looked at Hedy's rumpled clothes. "And Hedy," she added, "do yourself a favor, sweetie. Get rid of that sweatshirt. It came from Krock's General Store, didn't it? It fairly screams 'Fox Creek'—and that's *not* the fashion statement the world is waiting for, darling, trust me."

Jolene smiled again, turned, then strode briskly to her Mercedes. Hedy watched her pull out of the driveway and felt that same strange emptiness that had been haunting her ever since she had moved into the house.

She suddenly wondered if her master plan was really going to work. Perhaps she was foolish to think she could emulate Jolene in even the smallest way. She looked down at her old sweatshirt and faded jeans. She felt like a peasant, a hick with hayseeds in her hair. Perhaps she shouldn't have left Fox Creek at all.

Coward, said a corner of her mind that refused to quit. *Get to work.*

She went back inside and picked up her spray bottle of cleaner and her cleaning cloths. She got to work.

Security sat on the windowsill, an empty expression on her beautiful face. She kept staring out across the lawn at the hideous, earless Benchley, as if she were hopelessly smitten.

Hedy thought of Ty Marek and scrubbed the woodwork even more vigorously. Jolene's warning had been clear: Ty was a womanizer, irresponsible and dangerous. He was out of Hedy's league, someone best not even thought of.

"No way," Hedy warned Security, pointing out the window at the tomcat. "He's off limits. Strictly forbidden. This house ignores the Marek house—man *and* cat. Neither one is up to any good."

Security ignored her. Outside Ty Marek's cat whirled and danced like a dervish, showing off shamelessly in the autumn leaves.

It obviously took after its master. It didn't care what Hedy or anyone else deemed forbidden.

CHAPTER THREE

BY SIX O'CLOCK in the afternoon, Hedy decided that restoring an old house was every bit as backbreaking as running a farm. And she had not yet even begun the hard part—painting, papering, patching, ripping up carpets, and refinishing floors.

Too tired to eat, she freshened up by taking a shower and washing and blow-drying her hair. She put on another pair of worn jeans, another unfashionable sweatshirt by the absolutely inexclusive Krock's General Store of Fox Creek.

She dabbed on peach-colored lip gloss and examined herself in the bureau mirror. "Jolene's right," she told her reflection. "You've still got Fox Creek written all over you." She shrugged. So be it.

She marched to the kitchen to refill her scrub bucket. She would have to clean the years of dust from the carved railing of the staircase—a job that should only take about three hours, she thought grimly.

Scrub bucket and brushes in hand, she started purposefully toward the stairs. She stopped in midstride when a loud and restless knock shook her front door.

She felt suddenly cold all over and full of fluttering disquiet. That was Ty Marek's knock. She didn't question precisely how she knew it, but she did.

She pulled the door open. He stood there. As usual, an unruly wave of dark hair fell over his brow, but at least this time he was fully clothed. He wore khaki chino pants that hugged his long thighs and lean hips, and a flannel shirt of navy-and-white plaid.

Into his belt were thrust a hammer, a screwdriver, and a putty knife. He had a stained-glass window tucked under his arm as well as another package, almost as large, wrapped in white paper.

"It's your friendly neighborhood repairman," he announced, "here to replace your window. How lovely you are with your scrub bucket. If all cleaning women looked like you, I'd become a merchant of mops."

Hedy was torn between the unexpected turmoil caused by seeing him again and the desire to give back a comment as mocking as his own. Instead she clenched the handle of the bucket tighter, blinked hard and wondered if she was going mad. Behind Ty, a strange creature stood on her porch.

This time it was not a cat without ears. It was an overweight brown dog wearing a red knitted hat with a tassel on the top and a string tied under the chin.

"What's that?" she said, keeping her voice level. She pretended she wasn't the slightest bit unnerved by a fat dog with a hat tied on its head.

He glanced over his shoulder, his face impassive. "That? That's Mrs. Parker, my dog."

"Mrs. Parker?"

"Named for the great humorist Dorothy Parker. Benchley is named for her equally great cohort, Robert Benchley."

"That dog is wearing a *hat*," Hedy said accusingly.

"Mrs. Parker likes to ride in the convertible. She's part basset hound, and basset hounds have sensitive ears. I put a hat on her so she won't catch cold."

"How considerate," replied Hedy, not even trying to sound sincere.

"Listen," he returned, "when a man has one ear-related tragedy, like Benchley's, he becomes conscious of the auditory welfare of his other loved ones. Are you going to let me in, or do you want me to install this window on your porch swing?''

"Come in," Hedy said helplessly. "I don't even know why you're asking. You usually just walk in. How'd you get that window so fast, anyway?"

He pushed open the door. The fat dog stared after him, adoration in her eyes. Then she yawned and lay down so swiftly it was as if she had fallen over. She hit the porch with a thud.

"Actually," Ty said, "I've broken this window so many times, I keep one on order. With my friend Marcia. She runs a stained-glass shop."

Marcia, Hedy thought warily, adding the name to those of the Canarsi twins and Myra Rubicoff, with her famous muscle tone. Still another woman; Jolene was right about this man—he must be kept at a distance. "Don't order another one," Hedy warned coolly. "I don't want that window broken again. Ever."

"Put down that bucket, will you?" he requested, taking it from her. "I have the feeling you want to empty it on my head." He set the bucket down and walked to the broken window. Expertly he removed the old frame and installed the new window. It was, in every detail, an exact duplicate of the one he had broken.

He had it in place in a remarkably short time. Hedy was impressed in spite of herself. If Ty Marek ever wanted to give up writing, he had the potential to be a professional carpenter.

"You're good at that," she said grudgingly.

"Practice makes perfect. I have to take the old frame to Marcia so she can have another window on order."

He thrust the screwdriver back into his belt and gave her a slightly tilted smile. For no reason at all, Hedy's heart tilted as if in reply. She willed it to behave.

"Didn't I just say I never wanted this window broken again?" She sounded far sterner than she felt. Resisting the perilous Marek charm was proving more difficult than she'd thought.

"What we want," he drawled sardonically, "isn't always what we get. Of course, your cousin wouldn't tell you that. She thinks she'll always get what she wants. I saw her moneymobile parked in your driveway. A fine car, if you want to take your rightful place in society. I admired it from my wrongful place in society—my hammock."

Hedy's eyes flicked over him dubiously. "Your hammock? This is a weekday—don't you ever go to work?"

"I'm a writer," he bantered, mocking the seriousness of her tone. "I'm always working. Even in the hammock. Sometimes especially in the hammock. I'm even working now, as I gaze down into your scared, solemn and lovely face."

"Oh, really," muttered Hedy, turning away from him. The flannel shirt made his shoulders look too broad and leanly muscled. The stained-glass window was throwing a green shaft of light across his eyes that made them look more strange and enchanting than ever.

"But I *am* working," he insisted, stepping in front of her and capturing her gaze again. "I keep asking myself how to describe your eyes. And all I can think of is the first spring flowers—the ones so blue they're lavender. But 'violet eyes'? That's such a cliché. And your eyes aren't commonplace. Not at all."

"Stop that," Hedy breathed. No man had ever spoken to her this way before.

"No," he protested softly. He leaned his fist against the wall so that he had blocked any effective exit. "Never interrupt a man at his work. Your eyes. They keep reminding me of spring—the brave, first days of spring. But exactly what color are they? Maybe the shade of old-fashioned lilacs, or blue irises, or hyacinths—no, I'm still not getting it right. I'll have to look into them some more."

"Stop—*please*," Hedy almost cried. There was something close to desperation in her voice, and it brought a wariness into his expression.

He drew back slightly, but he reached out and fingered a strand of brown hair that fell softly to her shoulder. "I'm sorry," he said. His mouth quirked slightly as if he would say more, but he did not. He opened his fingers and reluctantly let the tendril of hair slip from his grasp. "I'll stop," he uttered at last. "For now. But I'll spend long hours in the hammock thinking about it, I guarantee you."

With a sigh of reluctance, he stepped back. He picked up the package he had set in the old armchair, thrusting it at Hedy without ceremony. "Here," he said casually. His mercurial mood had changed again. He seemed bored, almost tired of her. Hedy was more confused than before.

She held the package, which was heavy and tied up with string, staring at it foolishly.

"Open it," he ordered. He sank down onto the couch, stretched out his arms along its back, and crossed his long legs. He gave her a bemused glance, then turned his attention to Security, who lay on the carpet as lifelessly as a cushion.

Hedy pulled off the string and removed the paper. An antique mirror lay within, the twin of the one Ty had broken the day before. She exhaled sharply.

"How did you find this?" she asked, letting the last of the paper fall away. She held out the heavy mirror. It was indeed the undamaged replica of the one he had ruined.

"My friend Trena, the antique dealer," he answered in a jaded voice. "Trena's always resourceful. Is this cat all right? Sometimes I'm not sure it's real. You didn't let somebody palm off a false cat on you, did you?" He stared at the animal with thinly veiled dislike.

Trena, she thought grimly, *yet another woman.* Didn't this man know any other men? "The cat is fine," she answered stiffly. "She just isn't—demonstrative."

"Takes after you," he grumbled, still studying Security. The cat opened her yellow eyes and looked back as if she could see right through him.

"Thank you for fixing the window," she told him. She stood clutching the mirror nervously. The memory of his closeness still sent odd sensations dancing through her. She cursed him for it. There was no place for such unbidden feelings in her master plan. Especially about a man like this one.

He turned his attention from the cat to her. "Go out with me tonight," he said suddenly. "Now. Let's go."

She busied herself by taking down the broken mirror and hanging up the undamaged one.

"Don't be silly," she answered. She hoped he couldn't see the color flaring in her cheeks. She kept her back to him, but she could see his reflection in the mirror. His eyes, with their disturbing blend of mystery and merriment, were intent upon her.

"You didn't have to buy a new mirror," she said, brushing away his invitation. "It would have been enough to fix the old one."

"It was easier to buy one. That's not exactly a priceless heirloom, you know. I said, go out with me. Come on. Get a sweater or something. I'll show you downtown Chicago. I bet you haven't seen it yet."

The mirror in place, Hedy turned to face him. She felt self-conscious in her old jeans and sweatshirt, her face free of makeup and her hair tumbling unrestrained to her shoulders. "I couldn't possibly go."

He looked her up and down. "You're busy, eh?" He glanced around the room, then back at her. "This house'll keep you busy, too. For the next fifteen years. You'll have to take a break sooner or later, and it might as well be now. So let's go downtown. Wait—I know what you're going to say—you're not dressed for it."

"I'm not dressed for it," Hedy returned, as faithfully as an echo. She knew she couldn't be dressed for it even if she wanted to be. Yesterday's broken glass had ruined her one presentable blouse.

He ran a hand impatiently through his wavy hair. "Go the way you are. You look fine."

"Like this?" she asked in horror. She stretched out her arms slightly as if to demonstrate how impossible it would be.

"Exactly like that," he affirmed. "My sister Lilka's a fashion consultant at the Water Tower Mall. She says nothing beats the basics. One is never ill-dressed, says Lilka, in the simplicity of clean denim and the classic gray of the unadorned sweatshirt. I mean, they *pay* this woman for knowing stuff like this. And she's right. I don't know how you'd look any better."

Hedy blushed and almost smiled. She ducked her head slightly, but stole a glance at him. "Maybe your sister would think I'm a fashion plate—but most people wouldn't. I'm not dressed for downtown Chicago."

"Then you don't understand Chicago," he insisted. "Chicago is all things to all men, all women, and all clothing. If we wanted to wear diamonds from head to toe, there'd be a place to wear 'em. And there are places for jeans, lots of 'em, great ones. Chicago's never been a city to look down its nose. Come on, I'll show you the lights. And you can dim them with your luster."

"No," she said.

"Look," he reasoned. "We'll go to Old Town. That's the artsy section—jeans and sweatshirts are practically required there. It'll be bright and beautiful—shops and galleries, clubs and pubs and bars and cafés. And jazz. All waiting for you."

"No." She crossed her arms in embarrassment.

"I know a club," he went on convincingly. "It's the world's greatest club for music. It's a little place. The Silent Squire. They practically kick you out if you don't wear jeans. We can eat at a little Czech restaurant I know, where they don't serve anybody who isn't wearing jeans, and we'll still have plenty of time to catch the first show at The Silent Squire. How about it?"

Hedy ducked her head again in confusion. Listening to Ty's blandishments was altogether too pleasant. She remembered Jolene's warnings, her own misgivings. "No," she said for a third time. She didn't even know why he was asking. He probably didn't, either. He was a man who followed his impulses, no matter how wild or unseemly or spur-of-the-moment. She was a woman who could no longer afford impulses. Of any kind.

He sighed. He collapsed back on the couch, lounging against its farthest arm, watching her. Trying to ignore him, she picked up the bucket, carried it to the foot of the stairs and set it down smartly. She took the bottle of spray cleaner, aimed it at the carved top of the newel post and pulled the spray trigger.

"I don't believe this," he muttered from the couch. "It's after six o'clock. It's quitting time. It's a beauteous evening, calm and free. Winter's almost upon us and we have to gather these last precious, golden hours while we can. And you—you're going to give a banister a bath?"

"Yes," Hedy answered, scrubbing hard and not looking at him. "Because W. A. Tidwell obviously never did. He seems to have been a stranger to every cleaning device known to humanity."

"The man was ninety years old, for crying out loud," Ty retorted in disgust. "Unlike you, he didn't enjoy hanging from the ceiling by his knees and waging war on cobwebs. He had better things to do."

"Obviously." Hedy was scouring the dingy paint with an old toothbrush, but the dirt refused to budge.

"He had sunsets to watch," Ty went on, his voice animated by indignation. "He had autumnal breezes to sniff, and birds on the wing to watch. At night there were stars to count, and in the morning, there was the porch swing to sit in, and robins to listen to, and once in a while, a pretty girl who'd go by, to smile at..."

"Like the Canarsi twins, in their Spandex running outfits?" Hedy asked, never missing a stroke in her cleaning.

"No. To see the Canarsi twins, you have to go to the park. W.A. preferred to sit on the porch and wait for Mrs. Feboldson to come jogging along. A sign, alas, of his advancing age. When Mrs. Feboldson jogs, the earth moves. But you and I are young, as is the evening. Let's go. I am filled with the mounting and insurmountable desire to boogie."

She straightened up and put a sudsy hand on her hip. "Then go boogie. I'm busy. I don't boogie. And if I did, I don't think I'd do it with somebody like you."

He was nonplussed. He plumped up a sofa pillow and put it behind his dark head. He watched her work. "Why?" he asked. "What's wrong with me?"

She shot his recumbent form a derisive look, then went back to her scrubbing. "Your cat has no ears," she said. "Your dog wears a hat. If you work at all, you seem to do it in a hammock. Your house, I notice, is painted an unsightly orange—"

"Oh. That. I had a bet with a few of the boys at the *Trib* about the Illinois-Wisconsin game. I lost. I had to paint the house. You wouldn't want a gentleman to welsh on his bets, would you?"

"Somehow, I don't think a gentleman would be lying, uninvited, on my couch watching while I scrub my fingers to the bone."

"Sorry. I made a sacred vow to myself never again to do physical labor of any kind. It's like my promise never to walk more than five blocks. It's a question of honor."

"It's a question of lazy," Hedy replied with some spirit. "If you're tired, go home and lie down."

"W.A.'s place was always like a second home to me," he said, unfazed. "Many a time did I recline on this very couch. Only W.A., a much more sensible person than you, would be relaxing in his armchair and we'd be drinking beers and watching football on TV. You don't have a beer, do you? Preferably a nice, dark, German beer?"

"Sorry," she muttered. "You'll have to rough it."

He sighed. "The only way I'll get you out of here is to throw you over my shoulder like a caveman and carry you out, isn't it?"

She gave a curt nod. She kept on scrubbing.

"Ah," he said wearily. "I thought so. Let's get it over with, then."

With surprising alacrity he was on his feet. His long legs carried him to her side. He took the dripping scrub brush from her and dropped it neatly into the bucket. Before she knew what was happening, he had scooped her up and with one economical movement thrown her over his shoulder.

Hedy gasped. She was staring down at her carpet from the height of his shoulder. She opened her mouth but could say nothing. He held her in place as securely as if she were tied to him.

"A man's got to do what a man's got to do," he said in resignation. "Is this your purse? Are your keys in here?"

He took her silence for assent. He picked up her purse and threw the strap over his other shoulder. He stopped by the coatrack near the door. "That your jacket?" he asked, nodding at the short, red-and-black-plaid coat that hung there. "Grab it. I've got the top down on the car and it'll get cold."

Hedy was so dismayed that she obeyed without thinking. No man had picked her up in his arms since she was a child. To be hung over Ty Marek's shoulder so unceremoniously was both novel and perturbing. Hedy Hansen was trying hard to live like a serious young woman who always used her head. To be treated like this confounded her.

"Q-quit that! *Put—me—down,*" she managed to stammer. But he was already outside on the porch, locking her door. He patted her bejeaned hips comfortingly. "There, there," he said. "Play hard to get, and see what happens? Go home, Mrs. Parker."

He marched down the porch stairs. Helplessly, Hedy watched her house recede. The fat brown dog unhappily watched them go, then got to her feet and waddled dispiritedly toward Ty's house.

Ty went across her lawn and his own, past his house, which was larger and even more Victorian than Hedy's. "Put me down!" she ordered again. She wondered if she should beat on his back with her fists, like a woman in a film. "People will see!"

He shrugged, and she could feel the movement of his shoulder against her stomach. "So what?"

He was in his driveway now. He approached his car, a red Corvette convertible. The afternoon shadows were lengthening, the air growing slightly chill. Hedy thought again about beating on his back. She wondered if she should kick. But, she thought irrationally, this was supposed to be a good neighborhood, and she certainly didn't want to call attention to the situation. What if the neighbors *did* see?

Ty carried her to the passenger side. With another lightning-quick motion, he lowered her from his shoulder and swung her into the passenger seat of the Corvette.

He crossed to his own side, leaped into his seat without opening his door, reached over, drew the seat belt across her breasts and snapped it in place by her hip. Again, Hedy wondered if she should try to run away or scream for help.

Ty gunned the car backward out of the drive and after changing gears, hit the accelerator.

Hedy stared at him, aghast. "What if somebody saw us?" she managed to sputter. "They'd think we're both crazy!"

He cocked his head and checked the rearview mirror. "The neighbors? They're used to me," he said, as if that explained everything.

"Well, I'm not!" she exclaimed, the enormity of his actions sinking in. "Just what do you think you're doing, anyway?"

"Saving you."

"What?" Disbelief edged her voice.

"Saving you—from yourself." He gave her his exotic green-brown glance. "Tell me, just what is it that Fox Creek, Michigan, does to pretty blue-eyed girls?"

So that's it, Hedy thought, her dismay increasing. Perhaps Ty was using her to spite Jolene, just as Jolene had predicted. Or perhaps he had practically kidnapped her simply to prove he had the power to do it.

"Fox Creek doesn't do anything to its girls," she answered, struggling to be calm.

He swung the Corvette onto the Eisenhower Expressway with a combination of speed and daring that was positively frightening. There was bitterness in her voice. "The hell it doesn't," he said.

For once he didn't sound lighthearted at all.

CHAPTER FOUR

DOWNTOWN CHICAGO made Hedy feel as if she were Dorothy catching her first glimpse of the magic city of Oz. In the convertible, as millions of lights dazzled and enchanted her, she felt she was flying through a city made of wind and darkness and jewels.

Ty, softening slightly when he saw her genuine wonder, took her on a detour along Lakeshore Drive. The stretch along Lake Michigan was almost regal, with spacious parks and truly majestic buildings.

Near McCormick Place he turned back north, so Hedy could see it all again. The great buildings, bathed in light, made her feel slightly drunk with rapture. The elaborate Buckingham Fountain, shining with illumination, seemed to have come right out of a fairy tale.

The Old Town district, with its distinctive blend of Victorian and modern architecture, was just as exciting. Ty parked the car and they walked among the crowds on Wells Street.

They ate in a tiny but wonderful Czech restaurant, where, true to Ty's word, at least some of the clientele was in blue jeans. Old Town was one of those magical places where the poorest student and the richest citizen could rub elbows without self-consciousness: it belonged to everyone.

Hedy felt wonderfully sated after a supper of goulash and dumplings and apple strudel. She could have happily sat in the restaurant till dawn, dreamily remembering the tastes and scents and sights of the night. But as soon as she finished her coffee, Ty was on his feet, restless and ready to move.

Near the Garrick Theater, he led her up a steep flight of stairs to a tiny nightclub that was so dark that Hedy had to let him take her hand and lead her to a table. The club was Ty's beloved Silent Squire, and on its small stage, a beautiful young black woman sang.

Hedy immediately recognized the woman's husky, sensuous voice. "Good grief," she said, her eyes widening, "isn't that Diana Turner?"

Ty nodded and ordered a bottle of Bordeaux from the waiter who had appeared.

"Diana Turner's an important star," Hedy objected, her voice almost a whisper of awe. "What's she doing in this little place?"

"Singing," Ty answered, amused. "This is Chicago, Hedy. A great jazz center. This club's little, but it's important. Some of the best acts try out new material here."

As Hedy sipped her wine and listened to the provocative lilt of Diana Turner's music, she glanced around the dark room. Her eyes adjusted, and she saw that Ty had told the truth. Elegantly dressed couples sat next to others in faded jeans and college sweatshirts. Chicago could be either plain or fancy, or both at once if it chose. It was a city as independent as Ty Marek himself.

When the set ended and Diana Turner left the little stage, Hedy turned to Ty. His eyes were already on her, as if he had been watching her. "This is wonderful," she told him, a lump of gratitude in her throat.

"You know—" his voice was husky "—maybe it's a trick of light, Hedy, but you look happy." He studied her over the edge of his wineglass.

"I *am* happy," she answered, but turned her gaze from his. She was happy, but she was also suddenly overwhelmed by doubts. She shouldn't be here. She'd been warned about this man.

He put his hand over hers. She flinched. His fingers were strong and warm on her own, but she sensed danger in his touch.

Although she said nothing, he drew back. "Sorry," he said, sounding more harsh than apologetic. "I forgot. You're one of the ice maidens of Fox Creek. What is it—something in the water up there?"

She said nothing, still feeling the tingle where his hand had touched hers.

"I suppose Jolene told you we used to go together," he muttered. "Years ago, back when dinosaurs roamed the earth."

She nodded. She decided to be blunt. "She said you were in love with her. That you never got over her. That you'd become a sort of womanizer."

He gave an indifferent shrug. "Guilty, I suppose. On all three counts. She changed me, that's for damn sure."

Hedy didn't answer. He'd admitted the truth of all Jolene's accusations. Hedy's wariness intensified.

He appraised her, his face impassive. "You look just like her," he said almost gruffly. "The way she looked back then. Before she bleached her hair and put on all that makeup and got encrusted with jewels. And you seem determined to travel the same road she was bound to take—the one that leads you to success at any cost."

Hedy eyed him cautiously. His face was in shadows, but she could see that he looked untypically earnest, almost stern. "I don't understand why you brought me here," she said uneasily, "if I remind you so much of something you'd rather forget."

He shrugged again. "Who said it was bad? Jolene may have been the best thing that ever happened to me. But I keep seeing somebody besides Jolene in you. You remind me of my favorite person."

"Who?" she asked, truly puzzled.

"Me," he said, his voice almost grim. "Sometimes you remind me of me. When I was young and foolish. Or rather young and serious, which was even worse."

She opened her mouth but could say nothing.

"Look," he said, almost paternally, "you're a beautiful young thing. I sense laughter and warmth and all kinds of things locked up in you, wanting out. But for some reason you're afraid. You think you've got to be deadly serious—or monsters will get you."

Hedy was taken aback by his unexpected intensity. "What monsters?" she demanded, still feeling unsettled.

He stared moodily into his wineglass. "The monster of never having enough. The monster of loss. The monster of caring too much. The monsters of insecurity, fear and sometimes, unfortunately, greed."

He drained his glass and gave a sigh of exasperation. "Greed," he muttered. "That's the one I really hate."

"I don't understand." She was bewildered at the somber turn the conversation had taken.

He set down the glass. "You came to Chicago to make your fortune, right? Just like your cousin, the great real-estate heiress."

"Not my fortune," Hedy objected, "just a—a future, that's all."

"What's the matter with Fox Creek?" he challenged. "Has time stopped there? The future can't occur in Fox Creek? You have to come to Chicago to find it?"

Hedy didn't understand why he was acting so confrontational, almost combative. "What's wrong with coming to Chicago?" she fired back. "No, as a matter of fact, there wasn't any future in Fox Creek. None."

"And no past?" he demanded. "Nobody you hated to leave? No family? No friends? No man?"

Hedy retreated into a defensive silence. "Most of my family's gone from up there," she said at last. "The small farmer can hardly make it any more. You may think poverty's picturesque. You've obviously never experienced it."

"Neither have you," he retorted, "or you wouldn't be buying up pricey Chicago real estate. And paying too much for it."

"Oh, really," Hedy said in exasperation. He was impossible. He was opinionated, overbearing, and had a positively perverse genius for leaping to conclusions.

"I asked you about your friends back in Fox Creek," he persisted. "And the man. Or the men."

"I didn't have time for friends," she replied with asperity. "Or men. I had other things to do." And she had. She and her mother had carried that farm on their backs like a bone-crushing burden.

"'Other things,'" he mocked. "Like getting ahead. If you're really like Jolene, you've dedicated your life to getting ahead."

Hedy looked away, staring off into a dim corner. She hadn't dedicated her life to getting ahead. She had spent most of it trying to stay even.

He took her silence for assent.

"Hedy," he said, shaking his head, "there's more to life than money. And there's also more than work."

She stared at him in frustration. "Who are you to judge? You hate work. You've got enough money that you don't *have* to work. You can lie around all day composing smart things to say. I find it a little odd that you're lecturing *me*."

"I'm not lecturing you," he protested impatiently. "I'm trying to talk to you. You don't understand—"

"No," she said righteously. "*You* don't understand. I came here knowing what I want and what I have to do to get it. That doesn't make me a monster."

"I didn't say you were a monster," he remonstrated. "I said you were afraid of monsters. You've got some problems—"

"What problems?" she challenged, indignant.

"Anybody who hates Christmas, buys an overpriced cat with the personality of a beanbag, and then names the stupid thing Security, has problems. Any woman who's never had time for friends or men has problems. Any woman who works all day and then all night has problems. You're driven, kid. It's written all over you. And it isn't good for you."

She put her hands in her lap and clasped them together so hard her fingers felt numb. Why was he doing this to her? Was this technique designed to break down her defenses? If it was, he didn't know how strong her defenses were.

"All right," she answered, "I'm driven. So why bother with me? Why don't you just leave me alone?"

"An excellent question," he returned. He shook his head as if he were puzzled himself. "Maybe because there's something about you. You've still got a kind of innocence. And sweetness and fire, too. But they're threatened. As if you're an enchanted princess, a girl imprisoned in a tower—a girl who ought to be saved."

Ty's words were a bewildering mixture of accusation and flattery, attack and seduction. *Be careful,* she warned herself nervously. *Words are his business. He knows how to twist them, distort them, make them stand on their heads. He knows how to use them to control people, to make them feel what he wants.*

"At the same time," he persisted, shaking his head again, "I can't be sure. Maybe I just brought you here to find out. Who are you—a pretty, vulnerable young woman from Fox

Creek? The real article this time? Or another blue-eyed barracuda cleverly disguised as a girl?"

Hedy stirred uncomfortably. The power of his gaze, even in this darkness, was discomfitting. He was playing some complicated game with her. "I don't know why you're saying all this," she declared. "And I don't know what Jolene did to you, but if you're trying to take it out on me—"

He cut her off abruptly. "Forget Jolene. It's you I can't figure out. You come across as if you're wearing armor, but it seems full of holes. Big ones. You're acting like the dauntless entrepreneur, the hard-eyed businesswoman, but I'm not sure you have the slightest idea what you're doing."

"I know exactly what I'm doing," Hedy retorted with false certainty. "I've planned everything very carefully."

He gave her a mirthless smile. "Maybe you have. How did a poor little girl from Fox Creek get enough money to buy W.A.'s house? Because Jolene was asking a chunk of money for it—that I do know."

Hedy stared into her wineglass. She twirled its stem nervously between her fingers.

"My mother died," she answered at last. Her voice was sharp because she was struggling to keep it under control. "I inherited the tree farm. I sold it."

That was all she could bear to tell him. The memories almost choked her throat shut. She couldn't talk about them yet. She couldn't tell him how every year they had thought, *This is the year we'll make it,* and every year something happened: it was too dry or too wet or there was a blight or a fire. She didn't want to tell him that her mother had worked and worried herself to death. Or that she had died three days after Christmas, on the anniversary of Hedy's father's first heart attack. She stared off into the darkness again, fighting the tug of the memories.

"I'm sorry," he said. He actually sounded sympathetic.

Hedy bit her lip. She couldn't yet contend with her emotions, but she didn't want him, or anyone else, feeling sorry for her. "I sold the farm and I left it, and I never want to go back," she said harshly.

But that wasn't the whole truth, either. It wasn't that she didn't want to go back to Fox Creek. It was that it would be too painful to return.

He raised an eyebrow. "You just walked away from the old homestead, the family farm? Never looked back? Didn't even feel a twinge?"

"Right," she lied, not wanting him to know how many twinges she had suffered, continued to suffer. "I'm one of the famous Fox Creek ice maidens, remember?"

"All too well," he said sarcastically.

He refilled his glass. His tone was resigned. "No close family left there?"

"Not many," she said, as if it didn't matter much. Most, over the years, had given up farming and moved on, although they had stayed in the area and there were reunions and get-togethers. "There's my cousin Tippy. She lived with my mother and me while she finished her senior year after her family moved to Grand Rapids. But she hated the idea of leaving Fox Creek and got married before school was over. She and her husband are trying to work his parents' tree farm. She's my age and already has a baby and another one on the way. I don't see how they manage."

"But you'll make sure *you* manage," he offered cynically.

"Yes," she returned, wondering how he made it all sound so mechanical and heartless. "I intend to manage just fine."

He cocked one eyebrow skeptically. "I hope you didn't put everything you had into W.A.'s house. You'd be better off tearing it down than fixing it up, you know."

"Don't be so negative," Hedy answered. "I have a master plan. The house is only part of it."

He leaned his elbow on the small table and rested his chin on his fist. "A master plan. Fascinating. It includes a crumbling house and a cretinous cat—what else is in this magical scheme?"

"School," she answered emphatically. "I'll go to college. I'll get a teaching degree. There are always jobs for teachers—always. By the time I'm through, I should be finished fixing up the house, too. Then I'll sell it and buy another house and fix that one up. And another after that. And if I like breeding cats, I'll keep doing that, too."

He pretended to be impressed, but his mouth had an ironic quirk. "What do you intend to teach? House-fixing or cat-breeding?"

"Business," Hedy answered in her most businesslike tone. "That'll help me understand financing and selling the houses."

"Sounds great," he remarked without enthusiasm. "All you have to do is keep W.A.'s house from falling in on your head, hope your cat doesn't forget how to breathe, and take on four years of college—a snap. You should have been easy on yourself and stayed on the tree farm."

Hedy was hurt that her ambitions impressed him so little. "It only sounds hard to you because you lie in a hammock all day, keeping your sacred vow never to walk farther than six blocks."

"Five," he amended. "And writing is hard work. I sometimes sit at the typewriter for minutes at a time."

"You're incorrigible," she retorted.

"Nope, Polish. And you're a dreamer, Hedy. What's the matter? Afraid if you stayed around Fox Creek, you'd end up like your cousin Tippy, settling for love and a family instead of three cubic acres of money?"

She glanced at him resentfully. She loved Tippy, but she had no illusions about Tippy's life. Hedy had watched too many people in Fox Creek marry too young. Falling in love often meant giving up dreams for debts, trading hopes for hardships.

Ty watched the complex play of emotions on her face with scientific interest. "What's the matter?" he asked. "Did I hit a nerve? Is money more important than love? Than a family? Than even taking a night off to have fun?"

She thought of her father and mother, who had had so little in their short lives. She thought of Tippy and Norm, struggling against the same harsh odds her parents had faced. Tears stung her eyes. She turned to the darkened stage so he wouldn't see them. He'd already made up his mind about her, so what good would it do to refute him?

"Things are easy for you," she murmured, keeping her voice cool. "They've probably always been easy. You don't understand."

"You didn't answer," he accused. "If you had to choose between money and love, which would you choose?"

She said nothing. She supposed if she answered honestly, she would say "money," only because she knew how deadly its lack could be. Of love, other than for her family, she knew nothing. She had dated little. The boys of Fox Creek had found her reluctant to become involved.

"I see," he said when she kept her silence. He looked mildly disgusted, like a man who had expected little and got precisely that. "Come on. I'll take you home. You need sleep, so you can get to work on your great master plan."

There was an enthusiastic burst of applause as the stage lights blazed again and Diana Turner returned to their brightness. The band began and the singer launched into her own unusual version of "Diamonds Are a Girl's Best Friend." Somehow the woman made the bouncy lyrics sound infinitely sad and yearning.

"An appropriate tune for your exit," Ty whispered in her ear. The warmth of his breath paradoxically made her shiver.

They went down the dark stairs and back into the lights of Old Town. He put his hand on her arm and stopped her for a moment. She stood by a long window box of flowers that were dying in the chill wind.

He stared down at her, examining her in the flickering light of an overhead neon sign as she stood with her hands thrust deep into the pockets of her old black and red jacket. The wind tousled her long hair, brightened her pale cheeks.

Ty's green-brown eyes looked uncharacteristically troubled. He seemed about to say something, but did not. He merely shook his head as the wind stirred his wavy hair.

"What?" she asked him, almost defiantly.

"Some advice. You ought to use your heart more, instead of your head all the time. The heart's a muscle, Hedy. Like any other muscle, if you don't use it, it shrivels up and wastes away."

The words jarred her. They were precisely the opposite from what both her mother and Jolene had told her. And they were right. It was dangerous to use the heart. It was so so fragile, so breakable.

"I'd rather use my head," she returned. "What's the matter, do women who think frighten you? Is that why Jolene left you? Because she was too smart for you?"

"Forget it," he said, his patience clearly at an end. "Just forget it."

He put up the top of the convertible for the drive back to Holly Street. Hedy sat uncomfortably, staring out at the gray expressway. They had nothing more to say to each other.

She supposed it was for the best. They seemed to have been born to oppose each other. He disliked her. She distrusted him. It should have been simple. She wondered why it felt complex, tangled and painful instead.

He walked her to her door, despite her protests. The wind had risen, and she kept her head down as she mounted the stairs, fumbling in her purse for her key. Just as she found it and inserted it in the lock, she felt his hands on her shoulders.

He forced her to turn and look up at him. The streetlight on the corner gave his shadowy features a slightly golden cast. Suddenly his nearness seemed threatening in ways she could only begin to imagine. Her blood began to course wildly with a powerful mixture of fear and excitement.

"Thank you," she said, struggling to hide her perturbation. "It was nice—the dinner and the music and the city. I'll be too busy to see much of you from now on, and we really don't seem to get along, but I hope there are no hard feelings and—"

He bent, pulling her against his chest as he folded her in his arms. He pressed his lips down forcefully upon her parted ones. He seemed all height and warmth in the cool September night, and his arms felt like a long-sought haven suddenly discovered.

He held her as if he never meant to let her go. He kissed her as if he meant to kiss her forever, showing her all the things a kiss could mean. Hedy was jolted by the realization that she wouldn't mind if he did kiss her forever. The touch of his hands, the warmth of his face against hers were so pleasurable they dizzied her. Her reaction was as powerful as it was unexpected.

His mouth was both gentle and demanding, his arms possessive. She could not have escaped the embrace if she'd wanted to. It was as if she were locked to him by an overwhelming force.

But then his lips left hers, his arms released her. He took a step backward. She stared up at his dark form. She had trouble getting her breath. "What . . . ?" she tried to ask.

"That's for goodbye," he said, the familiar flippancy in his tone. "Goodbye to what won't be. Goodbye to a lot of things. Not least, to Hedy Hansen of Fox Creek, who was probably a nice girl once. But who's disappearing very quickly and turning into somebody cold and hard and narrow. Oh, I'll bedevil you from time to time. There's something in those eyes of yours that beg for trouble, and I'll be happy to comply. But, other than that, I think it's best that this is goodbye. Not good-night. Goodbye. The end."

He turned, sauntering down the stairs and off into the darkness. "Thanks for the laughs," he said over his shoulder. His tone was scathing.

Hedy, her face burning, struggled with the lock and opened the door into her dark house. She turned on a table lamp, then collapsed on the couch, hiding her face in her hands. Bitter memories of the past mingled with fear and confusion about the present.

Security drifted by, and Hedy scooped her up into her arms and hugged her tightly. The cat showed no response whatsoever, but Hedy buried her face in its luxuriant fur anyway, wanting to destroy all memory of the touch of Ty Marek's lips upon her own.

"I'm not what he thinks," she told the inert cat. "Everything he thinks about me is wrong. I have feelings—all kinds of them. Too many."

But Security didn't care one bit about any of those feelings. She yawned rudely in Hedy's unhappy face. Security apparently cared only for Security.

CHAPTER FIVE

HEDY WATCHED as September grew more mellow, then cooled and drifted into October. It seemed that suddenly the trees were bare and the ground awash in their fallen leaves. The evenings grew dark sooner, hazed with a special shade of smoky blue.

She had to fire up the ancient gas heater in the dining room. Contrary to Jolene's optimism, the heater didn't begin to warm the entire house. Hedy moved from her upstairs bedroom to the small downstairs one and still shivered all night. She wondered how she would ever afford to put in a central heating system on her limited budget.

She had arrived in Chicago just in time to enroll in night sessions at the university on Lake Shore Drive. Three nights a week she braved the traffic and drove downtown to attend.

Every time she saw the skyscrapers rising out of the prairie as if by magic, she thought of Ty Marek. Each time she saw the city stretching around her, a wonderland of lights, she remembered him and the disturbing evening they had shared.

Ty, true to his word, kept his distance. But she could not help seeing him. He was not precisely cold, nor was she. But he seemed determined to needle her, and the atmosphere between them was prickly and charged.

On warm afternoons he would be lying bare-chested in his hammock in the backyard. Sometimes he read, sometimes he scribbled on a yellow legal pad, sometimes he merely stared up at the clouds in the bright blue autumn sky.

Once, when Hedy was raking leaves, he took notice of her. "Having a good time?" he asked sarcastically. He lounged more comfortably in the depths of his hammock. His own yard was a scandal of fallen leaves.

"How can you just lie there?" she challenged. "Doing nothing?"

"I'm not doing 'nothing,'" he retorted languidly. "I'm studying autumn. I have to scrutinize the way the sunshine falls. I have to inhale every scent, record the crackle of every leaf."

"You'd hear a lot more crackles if you raked a few," Hedy observed disdainfully.

"Why should I? You rake enough for two people. Besides, I'm writing."

"You haven't got any paper," she pointed out. She had stopped working and stood staring over the hedge at him. He was shirtless and lay in perfect indolence, the hammock swaying slightly.

"I'm writing in my head," he told her smugly. He pointed to the spot where the wave of hair fell over his forehead. "I'm working up a storm."

"Ha," said Hedy.

"Ha, yourself," he replied. "I'm writing about this brief autumnal beauty—and how some people are too busy to see it. They'll lose it forever. To them, leaves aren't something to be looked at or smelled. They're only to be raked or some damn thing." He grimaced slightly when he said "raked." "Look at you," he muttered, giving her a disgusted glance. "You're sticking them in garbage bags. Hiding their brightness. Leaves should be allowed to roam free."

"Oh? Well, yours are roaming into my yard, where *I* have to rake them."

"Who says you have to?" he demanded, putting his hands behind his head. "Why don't you lie down in them and roll around? Burrow through them like a gopher? Throw them up into the air and let them fall on your head? Have some fun. I might come over and roll around with you."

"You're insufferable," Hedy stated with conviction.

"I do my best." He crooked a brow wickedly. "Besides, you need the provocation."

She moved to the front yard to work, so she wouldn't have to put up with him any longer. Not only was he insufferable, he gave her a funny, nagging pain in the region of her heart. He always made her feel as if she had lost something extremely valuable, but she wasn't sure what.

She felt the same uneasy sense of bewilderment whenever she read his column. It appeared regularly four times a week.

Meeting his thoughts and opinions in print always gave her an odd sensation. Mere words on paper should have been remote and impersonal. But when she read, she could hear his mocking voice, see his slanted smile. Once again she would feel that inexplicable sense of loss.

A week and a half after the leaf incident, his column gave her a particular shock. He had written of a perfect autumn day and about a woman so bent on scraping every last colorful leaf into a pile, then imprisoning each captured pile into a black bag, that she didn't see the beauty of the day itself. She only saw an irksome task.

Hedy's face burned, for she knew it was about her. He made her sound like some sort of workaholic or robot, moving blindly through life, never savoring it. She crumpled up the paper and buried it deep in the wastebasket.

It wasn't fair, she thought righteously. He mocked her for doing what she had to: working hard. He never mentioned the other side, that he had done nothing at all that day—

except lie around soaking up the sun and sniffing the leaf smoke.

But, she admitted grudgingly, Ty Marek had mastered one skill perfectly. He always seemed to be having a wonderful time. He apparently came from a large family, for on weekends his house teemed with laughing people. Many of them had his height, wavy hair, and slightly exotic eyes.

Hedy grew to hate the weekends. The more the Mareks laughed across the way, the emptier her big house seemed. Sometimes she saw Ty throw a glance at her house, and for a moment his face would look almost serious. She herself would look away then, feeling strange and lonely.

Things became worse when they clashed over the evergreen tree. The evergreen in her yard had bothered her from the beginning. It was a scraggly old spruce that had lost half its limbs and seemed host to every blight and pestilence known to treedom.

It reminded Hedy of all the disasters the tree farm had faced. It brought Christmas to mind, and any number of other things she preferred to forget. One bright October day she looked out the window at its sadly misshapen form and decided enough was enough. She would chop it down and put it out of its misery.

She looked every inch the girl from northern Michigan as she strode purposefully toward the gnarled old tree. She wore her oldest jeans, a blue checkered shirt, and carried W.A.'s rusty ax over her shoulder. After gauging the spruce's half-hollowed trunk with an expert eye, she drew back the ax and prepared to strike.

Then, suddenly, Ty was there. He had shot through his front door and sprinted to the tree with a speed truly impressive for a man devoted to sloth. He stepped in front of the tree, blocking her aim. He held up a hand to halt her.

"Hold it," he said. He wore chinos and a forest-green sweater. He was shoeless and stood in the crackling leaves in his stocking feet.

Hedy regarded him with displeased surprise. "What are you doing? Go away. Put on your shoes."

"What are *you* doing?" he demanded. "Murdering a defenseless tree? Put down that ax, you assassin."

Hedy glared at him, but put the ax on the ground and leaned one hand on its upright handle. She put her other hand on her hip. "This is no business of yours. The tree is diseased. It's half dead. It's unsightly."

"So?" Ty shot back. "Nobody's perfect."

"So," Hedy muttered, "nobody asked your opinion, either. This tree has spruce galls. It has spider mites. It has moth larvae. It has canker. It has rust. It has borers. It also has a hollow in its trunk that's going to kill it. What's more, there's a mole living in its roots. Its time is up. Will you stand back, please?"

"No," Ty said flatly. "W.A. planted this tree the year his grand-niece was born. It's forty years old. It was the first tree on this street to ever be decorated at Christmas. This tree is historic."

"It's also an eyesore," Hedy returned. "Furthermore, it's my eyesore, it's on my property, and it's coming down."

"Wrong." He took a step closer to her. "It's also partly on my property. It stays up."

Hedy eyed him suspiciously. "This is my tree," she argued. "It's in my yard. I mow around it."

Ty's expression was smug. "Wrong again. W.A. thought he planted it in your yard. It's actually exactly in the center of our property line. Half of it's mine. So hands off, ice maiden."

This man, Hedy thought darkly, had been sent by malign forces to drive her mad. She retaliated. "Fine," she retorted, narrowing her eyes. "I'll just chop down my half."

"Wrong. Touch it and I'll sue your pretty little bottom off. Ah. I see terror in your eyes. It's become an issue of money. So, 'Woodswoman, spare this tree. Touch not a single bough. In youth it hath sheltered me, And I'll protect it now.'"

Hedy suddenly wished she had several large, hostile lumberjacks with chain saws to do her bidding. "Why don't you get serious for once in your life?" she fumed. "This is a hideous tree. You might as well decorate a garbage can for Christmas."

"I did get serious with you once. It was a disaster. Stop being such a materialist. Can't you see this tree has inner beauty?"

"No. I can't see it for the outer ugliness."

"Why don't you lighten up? Mellow out? Be of good cheer? You're going to die of old age at twenty-two."

"And you'll die of terminal immaturity at thirty-five," Hedy grumbled, shouldering her ax and starting back to the house, defeated. If he was going to make a scene and insult her about the stupid tree, she'd ignore him. One good snowstorm would probably knock the tree over, anyway.

"Hey," he called after her. "You're not giving up, are you? We were establishing a nice rhythm here. I was just starting to enjoy myself. You're kind of good at this."

Hedy shot him an unamused glance over her left shoulder. "Enjoy yourself with the mites and the moths and the borers and the mole. I'm not fighting with a barefoot tree activist."

"It's your loss," he called after her, laughing.

"Go defend a termite," Hedy called back, refusing to look at him. "Go protect a stinkweed." He only laughed harder.

She stalked into the house. She was shaking. Why, she wondered, did the most insignificant argument with Ty

Marek sparkle with such odd excitement? He had the power to bewitch her, even when he was infuriating her.

He confounded her completely. It was as if part of her feared his free and irreverent spirit and another part needed the very things she feared. There was only one answer to such a conflict. She'd throw herself into her work even harder.

ONE NIGHT AT TEN O'CLOCK, Hedy had just returned from her English class, tired but happy. She had gotten the highest grade in the class on her midterm theme, and the professor had read it to the class. "Going to be a writer?" the professor had gently teased, handing back her paper. "You've got a gift for humor and a light touch. I didn't expect it. You always look so serious."

Hedy, unable to think of an appropriate answer, had simply blushed and looked more serious than ever. But half an hour later she was still basking in the professor's unexpected praise.

Then a knock shook the door. She opened it to find Ty standing there. He wore a green parka, open to show his flannel shirt beneath. As usual, a lock of hair fell over his forehead. And, as usual, his expression was mocking.

"Good evening. The Federal Express delivery man was trying to find you. I had to sign for this." He handed her a large package. "What is it?" he asked with false pleasantness, "Milady's pipe fittings? Her socket-wrench set? A nice sledgehammer perhaps? The better to knock down the occasional wall?"

Hedy took the package, trying not to show her annoyance. Ty stood in the open doorway, but she refused to ask him in, even though it was a bitterly cold night and the wind was rising.

"It's photographs," she said shortly. "My aunt said she was sending some. Thanks for your trouble. Good night."

She started to close the door. He blocked her way. "Wait. Don't you want a neighborly chat? How's the house-restoration business? The cat-breeding business? The business-of-getting-a-business-degree business? Do you ever stop working? Do you ever take time to stop and smell the roses?"

You like to taunt me, you devil, Hedy thought bleakly. *You just love it for some reason.* "The season for roses is over," she said firmly. "Mostly, I smell turpentine. And everything's just fine, thanks."

He cast a skeptical eye around her entryway. She was stripping off the stubborn layers of wallpaper. The walls were marred by cracked plaster and scabs of old paper. "Looks like a bomb went off in here," he observed.

"As they say," Hedy replied, "you don't make an omelet without breaking eggs. If you find the sight unsettling—"

He shrugged. "It doesn't upset me. I don't have to do it. But it looks like an unholy drag. Why do all this yourself? It's going to take forever. Hire somebody to do it. Like Jolene does."

His suggestion startled her. "What?"

He leaned indolently against the doorframe. He made a lazy gesture toward the entryway. "Pay somebody to do all this. The way Jolene does. What's the matter? You don't think she does all the work on all those houses herself, do you? And ruin her nails? You're not that naive, are you?"

Hedy stared up at him, slightly stunned. Surely he didn't mean that Jolene bought old houses and paid someone else to do *all* the work. Jolene did most of the labor and hired help only for the most difficult jobs; she was sure of it, positive. Jolene had always given the impression she had slaved her way to prosperity. "I—" she said, groping for words, "—I'm not afraid of work."

"No. You're afraid of play. That's worse. What do you do all day in this old barn? Are you gold-plating the walls, or what?"

"What do you care? And why? Does it make you nervous, seeing somebody actually working?"

He crossed his arms and stared down at her sternly. "This particular misconception of yours has got to end. I happen to work hard. Did you ever try writing four columns a week? It makes you sweat blood."

"So far," Hedy sniffed, "I haven't even seen you sweat sweat. You always claim you're working while you're flat on your back staring off into space."

"Dammit," Ty returned indignantly. "Being funny is no joke. Do you ever read what I write?"

"No," Hedy lied blithely. "I don't have time. I'm gold-plating my house, remember?"

"I was once as deadly serious as you," he muttered. "Before I grew into the happy, shallow, frivolous, and uncommitted person you see before you now. Shallow and uncommitted as I am, though, I still have this urge to save you from yourself. Want to come over and get in the hot tub with me? I'll massage your funnybone. Very tenderly."

This was too much. This was adding insult to injury and then some. "Good night," Hedy said in a tone she hoped conveyed disdain. He gave her his superior half smile.

She shut the door and locked it with an emphatic click. She looked down at the Federal Express package in her hands and suddenly had the irrational urge to bury her face in the envelope and either laugh or cry. Why did she always bring out the absolute worst in Ty Marek? And he the worst in her? She'd never had such a disturbing relationship with anyone in her life.

She sat down on the sofa and rubbed her forehead tiredly.

The worst thing, she had to admit unhappily, was that in spite of everything she found him attractive. They clashed every time they met, they had clashed from the moment they'd met, they could barely stand each other. Yet the night he had kissed her, it had seemed for a magical instant that something far stronger than all their differences drew them together, almost against their wills.

No, Hedy thought, that was insane. He was not for her. Jolene had warned her. He had as much as told her so himself. Her own common sense cautioned her to keep her guard up. She would be a fool to be charmed by such a man.

She looked around the room. It did look as if a bomb had gone off. Her earlier triumph in night class faded away as apprehension overwhelmed her. Ty had planted a seed of doubt, and now it flowered with sinister blooms. She wondered exactly how much work Jolene actually did on the houses she restored. Jolene, after all, had always had rich husbands to fall back on if needed. Was Hedy taking on a challenge that was beyond the power of one inexperienced woman with little money?

The house itself suddenly seemed hostile, a monster that gobbled up her money and labor and demanded still more. Everything was costing more and taking longer than she'd planned, and somewhere, somehow, she was going to have to come up with the money to put in a decent heating system.

All that, and she had three classes to study for, as well. Suddenly she wished she had never left Fox Creek.

No, she thought determinedly. She couldn't afford self-pity any more than she could afford frivolity or wasted time. *Quitters never win,* she told herself firmly.

Almost mechanically, she opened the package her aunt had sent her. Aunt Priscilla was her father's sister and Jolene's mother. She lived in Sarasota, Florida, now. Hedy was touched to see that her aunt had put all the snapshots into a special album, a very expensive one.

She had enclosed a note, as well.

Dear Hedy, I'm so ashamed it took me so long to find these. I hope you're enjoying your wonderful new home. Jolene says she found a real jewel for you. But then she's always been a clever girl! Do I sound like a proud mama? I am! Uncle Harold sends his love. Tell our pretty Jolene hello from Mommy and Daddy.

Love and Kisses,
Aunt Priscilla

Hedy smiled. It was kind of her aunt to send the pictures, and she sounded the same as ever: bubbly, vague, and almost obsessively proud of her accomplished daughter.

Without thinking, Hedy opened the photo album. Her heart wrenched as soon as she saw the first page. She knew, immediately, that she had made a mistake.

There, in picture after picture, she saw the small happy family that had once been hers. There was her father with his beautiful eyes and infectious smile, grinning into the camera, his arm around Hedy's mother, who looked young, happy, and carefree.

There were pictures of Hedy as a child, clowning happily with either her father or mother or both, or all by herself, acting silly for the camera. There she was, entering her teens, suddenly self-conscious, but still looking mischievous. In one photo she was behind her father on the tractor, sticking two fingers up behind his head as if they were rabbit ears. He had a knowing, good-humored look on his face that clearly said he understood all too well what his playful daughter was up to.

And then her father disappeared from the pictures and there were fewer of them. Suddenly only she and her mother appeared in the photos. They usually had their arms around each other, smiling. But her mother looked older and changed somehow.

Hedy studied the backgrounds. The tree farm in winter, the trees dark against the snow. The inside of the house. The kitchen that she and her mother had painted and tiled together. The living room the two of them had papered, laughing at the mess the paste made.

Then the pictures ended abruptly, the album only half-full. Hedy blinked hard. There were no more pictures because there was no more family. Now there was only her.

She fought against admitting the reality of it and turned back to the front of the album again, to see her father and her mother together and young again.

She was startled to discover she was crying. The photos blurred before her. She sat with her hand over her eyes, silently weeping. She hadn't cried since her mother's funeral, hadn't allowed herself to do it. Suddenly she missed her mother terribly. She could have faced this task with her mother at her side. But she was alone.

She fought to regain her self-control. She straightened up and spoke aloud to herself. "It doesn't do any good to feel sorry for yourself," she said sharply. "It doesn't do one bit of good. Feeling sorry for yourself is stupid. It's stupid, it's stupid, it's stupid!"

She wiped her eyes angrily. Neither her mother nor her father would want her to react this way. She would have to be harder in order to survive. Well, she would survive, no matter how much hardness it took.

Another knock at the door jarred her. She felt alarmed and guilty, as if she had been caught doing something wrong. It sounded like Ty's usual impatient knock, but what could he want? He was the last person she wanted to see.

The impatient pounding shattered the silence again. "All right, all right." She rose, shutting the album and thrusting it under a sofa pillow. Hurriedly she wiped her eyes.

She pulled the door open. It was Ty again. He wore his unzipped dark green parka and was holding something beneath it. His breath plumed up into the night air. He looked half-angry.

"What do you want?" she demanded, her voice still shaky. She tried to reestablish her shattered defenses. She took a deep breath. She suddenly knew why he bothered her so much. He reminded her of happier days. Once upon a time her carefree spirit would have been a match for his own.

This time he didn't stay outside. He stepped in from the cold without being asked. "It isn't worth crying over, for Pete's sake," he said gruffly. He shut the door behind him to keep out the blast of frigid wind.

"Who's crying?" she asked, her chin up. "What's not worth crying about?"

"This four-footed fuzz-ball," he grumbled and withdrew Security from the folds of his parka. He had her by the scruff of her neck, and she hung there limply, looking at Hedy with her familiar empty expression.

"Security!" she cried, taking the cat. "How did you get her? When did she get out?"

"What?" Ty said in disbelief, his brows lowering. "You didn't know she was gone?"

"No." Hedy almost groaned. She had been so distracted she hadn't even noticed the cat had disappeared.

"She probably slipped out while you were insulting me earlier," he muttered. "You were too busy heaping abuse on my head to notice."

"Me?" Hedy objected. She was starting to pull herself together. She knew she needed to with him around. "You were the one who was insulting *me*, as I recall. As usual."

"You could say thank you, you know," he chided. "I've been out chasing these cats around the yard like a crazy man. And it's cold out there. You could at least offer me a cup of coffee or something. I nearly froze my ascot off."

"You're not wearing an ascot."

He looked down at his brown-and-white flannel shirt in concern. "Then it *did* freeze off. Come on, Hedy. Coffee—have a heart."

"Oh, all right," she said, too exhausted to argue. "But it's going to have to be instant again."

"Oh, well, my taste buds are frostbitten. It won't matter."

He followed her into the kitchen.

"Did you say 'cats'?" she asked, turning on the kettle. "That you were chasing cats, plural?"

He sat down at the table. He blew on his fingers and rubbed them together. "Yes. That fluff-brain and Benchley. I don't know if he was chasing her or she was chasing him. Anyway, I had to chase them both. *Me*—a man of my dignity and position."

Hedy looked down at him sternly. "I hope your cat didn't have an amorous gleam in his beady little eyes."

Ty shrugged. His shoulders looked remarkably wide in the dark green parka. "Benchley always has an amorous gleam in his beady little eyes. He and I are alike that way."

"Look," Hedy said, trying to sound stern, "I told you to keep that—that *thing* away from my cat. She's a valuable animal."

"And I told you I wouldn't be responsible," he retorted. "You let her out."

"They didn't—they didn't—the two of them—you know..." Hedy said, unable even to say such a terrible thing.

"Consummate their relationship?" Ty supplied with ironic delicacy. "How do I know? How do you even tell? Is Benchley supposed to lie back with a smile on his face, have a cigarette and say, 'Was it good for you, too, baby?'"

"Oh, really," Hedy said, truly embarrassed. "He'd just better not have done anything, that's all."

She poured hot water into two mugs and unceremoniously stirred in the instant coffee. She set the mug before him with a thump. She sat down across from him. The green coat made his eyes look greener than usual. When he raised the cup to his lips, she noticed his hand was scratched.

"Oh, no," she exclaimed. "She scratched you, didn't she? I'm sorry. I'll get some antiseptic."

"*Your* cat?" he asked sarcastically. "No way. It was Benchley. He tried to punch me out for ruining his plans. Can't say I blame him."

Hedy rose and went to the bathroom to get the antiseptic and Band-Aids. She brought soap and a washcloth, as well. "Here," she ordered, "let me clean you off. Animal scratches can be dangerous, especially from that creature of yours. His germs are probably mutants."

"My," he observed, looking up at her with an ironic grin, "aren't we the good little nurse? You've got a nice touch. Maybe I'll go out and get scratched again."

"Save your energy," Hedy warned him sweetly. "You don't want to lose too much blood. You wouldn't be able to saunter to the park to leer at the—who are they?"

"The Canarsi twins. In their wonderful skintight Spandex running outfits."

"Right," Hedy agreed, her mouth slanting in disgust. She dabbed on the antiseptic.

"Ooh. Ouch," he said without much sincerity. "Ouch. That smarts. Maybe you should kiss it and make it better."

She tried to ignore him. The mention of kissing disturbed her, even though he was joking.

"Let me see your other hand," she said briskly. He didn't comply, so she seized and examined it. "Oh, Ty," she said in true exasperation. "This one's worse. How'd you get so torn up?" There were only two scratches, but they were deep and ragged.

"I had to separate them," he admitted between gritted teeth. "They were kind of rolling around together in the leaves."

"Oh, no." Hedy's whole skull started to ache. Security couldn't have mated with that revolting evil-eyed cat. She just couldn't have.

In silence, she bathed his hand, swabbed on the antiseptic, and applied Band-Aids. "There," she said. "You'll live."

She began to move away, but he caught her hand in his bandaged one. "It still hurts. Hold my hand. Help me bear it. I think I can be brave if you're near me."

"You're not in *that* much pain." She tried to give him her severest look, but she had the feeling she failed and that her face told him something else instead.

"Right," he answered, his own face suddenly serious. "But you were. Why were you crying, if it wasn't about the cat?"

She tried to draw away but he held her fast. "I wasn't crying," she said. She didn't want to look at him. She realized the tear tracks were probably still clear on her face.

"Yes, you were." A shadow crossed his face. "Hey, it wasn't because of me, was it? I mean, I'm hard on you sometimes, but you always give as good as you get. I even had the feeling you kind of enjoyed sparring. In my family everybody teases everybody else—I didn't hurt your feelings, did I? Earlier, I mean?"

There he was, Hedy thought hopelessly, undergoing another of his bewildering transformations. He could be contentious, he could be flirtatious, but it was always worst when he was kind. "No." She shook her head, unwilling to admit he had been part of the problem. "It wasn't you."

He looked more concerned still, which made Hedy even more confused. "Well, something hurt you. I think it's still hurting. Come here and tell me about it." Gently he pulled her closer to him. "If you need a cry, I've got a good shoulder for it. In fact, it's so great, I ordered a second one—I've got a set. You can take your pick."

She smiled in spite of herself. He could always work a peculiar magic on her, and he was working it now. There was something in his smile that seemed to dissolve her doubts, banish her fears.

There was something in his touch, as well. Her hand felt wonderful in his, perfect, in fact. It seemed to fit exactly, as if the two of them had formed some important connection. It made her want to stop resisting him.

"I can't really talk about it. It's just—things get to you sometimes," she murmured. "You know. They keep mounting up. Then, all of a sudden, you just can't—resist—any longer."

"I know." With his other hand he traced the smooth curve of her inner forearm. "All of a sudden, you just can't—resist."

With a movement as sudden as it was unexpected he pulled her down to him, so that she was sitting on his lap. "You just," he repeated softly, "can't resist."

He looked in her wary eyes. His nearness and warmth heightened the dizzy confusion of her senses. He tightened his embrace, forcing her more securely into the crook of his arm. His other hand rested on her shoulder, his thumb touching the base of her throat so softly it was like a caress.

He took a deep breath. She couldn't seem to breathe at all.

With great deliberation, very slowly, he placed his lips on hers. He kissed her gently at first, and then with increasing demand. The sparkles dancing within Hedy seemed to explode silently into fountains of light. His hands began to move over her back and arms with increasing hunger.

Standing up, he pulled her more tightly to him, so that her body was firmly nestled against his between the open halves of his parka. Her breasts were molded against the hardness of his chest. The ardor of his mouth grew more fierce, rousing Hedy to yearnings of her own. Her hands rested on his shoulders, and she wanted nothing more than to be closer to him still.

She let her hands slip under his parka, to rest on the warm flannel covering his shoulders. He felt so completely right to her that she started to put her own arms around his neck. She was kissing him back with a fervency and a heat she had not known was in her.

All the warnings she had heard about him seemed to dissolve in the heat of his embrace. All her misgivings about him melted away, and the coldness that had lived for so long in her bones melted, as well. She was in Ty Marek's arms, and it seemed a most desirable place to be.

Yet when Ty's hand boldly touched one of her breasts, her wariness returned with a start. What was she doing? He had caught her in an unguarded moment and she had fallen into his arms. She was on the edge of making love—to a man who didn't even like her.

The realization made her go as still and cold as stone. The warmth within her fled. She pushed herself away from his chest, breaking the kiss. His hand was still touching her breast, and it seemed to burn through her shirt.

She stared up at him, wanting to trust him but knowing she did not dare. But still she did not force his hand away.

His green-brown eyes burned down into hers. "I want to make love to you," he said. His voice was low and rough, strained with control. "I want to do it slowly and carefully and all night long. Then I'm going to want to do it again. And probably again."

Truly frightened, Hedy wrenched out of his embrace. Events were moving too fast for her; her emotions were out of control, and Ty Marek kept changing like one of those mythical creatures who could alter his shape at will. In the course of one night he had progressed from coldness through easy banter to all-out seduction.

She took a step backward. She could feel her lips throbbing with the hunger he had awakened, her pulses thudding with both desire and alarm.

She looked around her shabby kitchen and swallowed hard. She ran a hand through her tousled hair, then glanced at her jeans and worn tennis shoes. Why was he settling for the likes of her? she wondered. Out of lust or simple boredom, or a combination of the two?

"Go away," she said, her voice trembling.

He stepped toward her. "Hedy," he whispered, "what's wrong? I'm sorry. I didn't mean to hurry you. But—"

"Go away. Now. Please," she cried. And then, because she was ashamed of how fervently she had responded to him, she added, "I don't want to be anybody's toy. So leave. Now."

He looked down at her for a long moment. Conflicting emotions passed over his face. "A toy. Is that how you think I see you? After all these weeks? Look, Hedy, why don't we be honest for once? We want to go to bed together and that's that. Nobody's using anybody. It's a mutual giving. It's what we both want."

"No," she protested. He made it sound too simple, a casual thing without meaning or consequences. "It's *not* what I want. I don't want any such—giving. And I can do without that kind of receiving—thanks."

He regarded her cynically. "Then what do you want? Some rich old guy to feather your nest? Like your admirable cousin?"

"I just want to fix up this house myself and sell it. I don't want anybody—anybody at all."

"Right. You don't want anybody. You just want things. No wonder you don't like Christmas. The idea of giving must really hurt."

"I think you'd have more decency—" Hedy began, deeply wounded.

"Decency?" He laughed. "I thought I'd have more sense."

"Sense?" she asked, her heart beating fast.

"More sense than to bother with you," he answered scornfully. "Women like you don't like love. Women like you take a grand passion and make it petty—a matter of dollars and cents."

Breathing hard, Hedy studied the unfamiliar harshness in his face. "Love isn't petty," she said.

He laughed again. "Why, Hedy," he demanded, smiling bitterly, "how would you ever know? Who did you ever love? And who, in his right mind, would love you?"

CHAPTER SIX

SOMEBODY LOVES ME, Hedy thought, happily opening her mail. The ugly exchange with Ty Marek had marred her week, but today a fat package had arrived from her cousin Tippy. Happily Hedy curled up on the couch, determined to forget Ty and enjoy Tippy's letter. Tippy had sent a present, as well, a set of embroidered dish towels it must have taken her weeks to make. "For the new house," she had written on the card. "Hope they can live up to it."

Hedy felt a wave of homesickness as she read the letter. She missed Tippy and her family more than anything else in Fox Creek.

Dear Hedy,

We're hoping sales are really good this year. The trees looked really great. But it'd be nice to have Christmas be a holiday, and *not* the time of year when we find out whether we're going to be declaring bankruptcy. Well, that's one story you know by heart, right?

I know this year will be hard on you, remembering your mother. Remembering makes me sad, too. But if you change your mind and want to celebrate, come up and do it with us. It won't be fancy, but you'll be more than welcome.

Stay well, Hedy, and don't work too hard. We wish you the best of everything and appreciate all you've done for us. The two thousand dollars you *loaned* us when you sold the farm saved us—it really did. But I say "loaned," because no matter what you say, we can't accept it as a gift. We're going to pay you back as soon as possible. That's a promise! Happy New Home!

Love from all,
Tip

P.S. I'm so pregnant-looking, I'd swear it was twins this time, but the doctor says no—and he'd better be right!

Hedy read the letter again, and then again. For a moment she could almost smell the tang of Christmas pines, imagine the warmth of the farmhouse kitchen, the scent of baking sugar cookies. Although she had a class to study for, for once she put it off. She wanted to answer Tippy immediately.

She would make it clear that the dish towels were absolutely the most beautiful things in her old kitchen—indeed, the only beautiful things.

Hedy also had to tell Tippy that she would not return to Fox Creek for Christmas. Her hurt was still too raw. She wished she could convince Tippy and Norm she didn't want them to pay back the two thousand dollars she had given them. It had been a gift, pure and simple. The best gift they could bestow in return would be to let her forget there was such a holiday as Christmas.

The phone started ringing insistently just as she finished the letter. She hoped it was Jolene, from whom she seldom heard. She was alone in a strange city, and a familiar voice would be welcome.

But instead of Jolene's assured, velvety tones, she heard the ironical voice of Ty Marek. "Greetings," he muttered. "Better yet, Season's Greetings. Christmas is upon us. Unfortunately, I'm chairman of this year's Christmas committee. This means I call up everybody in the neighborhood and ask for twenty-five bucks. We need a new sign."

"What?" Hedy asked, horrified. She had just been writing to Tippy that she couldn't yet face the thought of Christmas. "Twenty-five dollars? For a sign?" Ty had been so unkind the other night she couldn't resist taking a jab at him. "What kind of sign? Are you gold-plating it?"

"Come off it," he snapped. "I don't care if they hang an old sheet up that says Welcome. But the women want the works, a new sign, professional quality—flashing lights and all that. Also new decorations for the new street lamps."

"I told you," Hedy said scornfully, "I don't like Christmas."

"Who cares what you like?" he countered. "This is a neighborhood project. A neighborhood *responsibility*. People come from miles around to see this street. Hundreds of kids expect it to be lit up. No, probably thousands. So cough up your share. Twenty-five bucks, blue eyes."

"I told you," Hedy repeated stonily, setting her jaw, "I don't celebrate Christmas. Have the party without me."

"And I said," he practically snarled in her ear, "this is a neighborhood project. Not everybody on this street celebrates Christmas privately, either. The Golds are Jewish. The Hongs are Buddhists. The Browns aren't any particular religion. But everybody gets into the general spirit—neighborliness, peace and good will. You can't object to that."

He's doing it again, Hedy thought bitterly. He's convincing me I'm wrong and he knows everything. He couldn't understand that Christmas was a trauma for her, one so deep she could not yet even bring herself to discuss it. Every year it had brought not good tidings, but bad ones, more debt and new failures. It was not, in any way, the season for her to be jolly.

"Look," he continued when she stayed silent. "Maybe you have problems with Christmas. But can't you just go along with it? It's a nice gesture, that's all."

"No," Hedy said, her voice choked with resentment and sorrow. "I don't want to."

"It's only twenty-five dollars," he chided. "Everybody's got twenty-five dollars to spare."

"I don't," she told him sharply. "You probably have bushels of money to throw around—everybody in this neighborhood probably does. But I *don't*."

He swore an oath that had little to do with neighborliness, peace, or good will. "I'll put the money in for you, you tightwad."

"Don't you dare," cried Hedy.

"I'll put in fifty dollars in your name," he gibed. "Maybe a hundred. Maybe five hundred. Do you know why? To shame you. If it's possible."

Hedy felt her face grow hot. Why was he suddenly so holier-than-thou? Since when had he been Mister Public Spirit?

But she didn't have a chance to ask. He whistled a line of "Rudolph the Red Nose Reindeer" and hung up on her.

HEDY'S HUMILIATION INCREASED when, the next evening, three of her new neighbors came calling: Mrs. Gold, Mrs. Hong, and Mrs. Melrose.

Mrs. Gold was a small, round, graying woman who looked designed to be hugged. Mrs. Hong was tall and stately, with beautiful blue-black hair piled on top of her head. Mrs. Melrose was a young woman with flaming red hair, cut in a pixie cut, and when she smiled, her freckles all seemed to change places and do a complicated dance.

"We're tardy," said Mrs. Melrose, after she'd introduced the three of them, "we should have welcomed you long ago, but—" She gave an apologetic shrug.

"My Joe, my husband, was sick," explained Mrs. Gold. "Such complications with his gallbladder operation. Also, my daughter Beverly got herself engaged. What a fuss!"

"I teach at the high school," Mrs. Hong said, her precise voice slightly accented. "Math. The new semester was starting when you came. Madness—always."

"And I have four kids, a new poodle I can't housebreak and I backed the convertible into the fish truck at the supermarket. Ever get a whiplashed neck *and* your car full of live shrimp? That's living, honey." Mrs. Melrose grinned, obviously the kind of woman who thrived on action.

"Won't you come in?" Hedy asked, holding the door open. "I don't have real coffee, but I can offer you instant."

"No, thank you," Mrs. Hong answered politely. "It's obvious you're busy. We can't help but see how hard you work. We didn't come to interrupt."

"No," Mrs. Gold announced, "We came to thank you. Ty said you donated five hundred dollars to the fund for the new Christmas sign."

Hedy blinked in horrified surprise. He had actually done it. "But—" she began, embarrassed.

Mrs. Melrose's freckles danced as she smiled, "No buts about it—that's generosity with a capital G. That gives us a lot more money than we need."

"So we're giving the extra to a fund for the needy," Mrs. Gold told her. "And we're going to have a decent sign at last. That old banner is so full of moth holes it should have fallen apart years ago."

"And Ty asked me to give you a receipt—for your taxes," twinkled Mrs. Melrose. "I'm the committee's treasurer. Here it is."

Hedy tried to wave away the receipt.

"You take that," Mrs. Gold insisted. "No nonsense. You take it. And thank you so much. You're going to fit right in here, I can tell."

"Listen," Hedy said desperately, feeling terrible. "I can't take credit for this—I didn't—I wouldn't—"

"Ty Marek said you would be modest." Mrs. Hong smiled. "He said you'd deny it."

"But all that money—I didn't—" Hedy wailed.

Mrs. Gold cut her off. "He said you didn't want people to know. That you made sacrifices. Well, we know and we thank you. And we wish you a happy season and hope we'll all grow to be good friends. I brought you some brownies, by the way," she added, handing her a covered plate. "A belated welcome gift."

"Oh, thank you," Hedy murmured in confusion, "but don't give me credit for that donation. I didn't make it. Somebody else put in the money in my name—in fact it was—"

"I know what you're going to say," interrupted Mrs. Melrose, looking jaunty, as if she knew all the neighborhood secrets. "Ty told us you'd try to wiggle out of it, even say he did it. Well, he said not to let you fool us. 'That girl is bursting with Christmas spirit,' he said. 'Just too modest to admit it. She doesn't want to look as if she's showing off.'"

"I..." Hedy began again helplessly. She felt like a miserly worm.

"I brought you some pecan clusters," Mrs. Melrose said, thrusting a tin at her. "The kids helped me make them. I hope you don't find the pet turtle in there."

"But I can't..." Hedy murmured, almost in tears.

"We're late, but our offer of friendship is sincere," Mrs. Hong said with gentle authority. "I hope you like tea. I've brought you a box of oolong. Welcome to the neighborhood."

"And thank you again for your neighborly spirit," Mrs. Gold finished warmly.

Hedy took the gifts helplessly. The three women said their goodbyes and started down the block. Ty came out of his house. He was wearing his green parka. Mrs. Parker, the overweight dog, waddled behind him, wearing the red hat with the tassel. He gave the women a mock bow, and they all giggled with pleasure, even the staid Mrs. Hong.

"Evening, ladies," he said. "Just taking Mrs. Parker for her constitutional. Her weight problem, you know."

He stopped on Hedy's front walk. He looked at the gifts in her hands and the mortified expression on her face. "Good evening," he said with another bow. "I see you've cleaned up in the gift department. Word of your neighborly spirit is already legendary. Did Emma Gold make you brownies? She must think you're something special."

Hedy glowered at him, and at his dog for good measure. "You fiend," she managed to choke out. "You scheming fiend. Those women think I'm practically Kris Kringle himself—how can I tell them the truth?"

He shrugged, his hair tossing in the cool wind. "You can't. Not without ruining the great impression you just made. You'd look like a two-faced skinflint. A miserly crab. People would cross to the other side of the street when they saw you. Children would taunt you. Dogs would growl. Cats would hiss."

"I can't take credit for something I didn't do," Hedy said furiously. "It's wrong. And I can't pay you back for—for I don't know how long. And I didn't want to give money in the first place."

He nodded, turning up his coat collar as the wind rose. "You don't owe me anything. I did it for the good of the neighborhood. People were starting to talk about you. You haven't been very friendly. Your image needed work. If it'll make people happy to think you're generous to a fault, I'm glad to make people happy."

He smiled. Mrs. Parker looked up at him with adoring eyes. She wagged her tail.

"You," Hedy accused, her heart beating perilously fast, "aren't doing this for kindness. You're doing it for spite. You twist everything so it sounds the way you want, you don't stop at anything, and you're devious and ruthless and diabolical."

"Yeah," he replied with a grin. "And I'm good at it, too." He cocked an impudent eyebrow. "Good night. And fa-la-la-la-la." He made a chucking noise to the dog and walked off into the evening shadows.

Hedy closed the door, shaking with anger and cold. She had stood in the doorway so long that her teeth were chattering. She set down her gifts on the table and went to stand by the old heater.

She stared at the gifts the three women had brought her. Tears stung her eyes. How dare Ty Marek put her in this impossible position? She had tried to tell the truth about the money, but nobody believed her. And if she did convince people of the truth, they would see her just as Ty predicted: an unfriendly miser.

The unshed tears made her throat knot with shame. Had people really started to think she was stuck-up and unfriendly? Had they been talking about her? It was true she hadn't tried to mingle with the neighbors. She had made no overtures of friendship, not one.

But couldn't Ty understand that she was frightened? Everyone else in the neighborhood seemed so settled, so confident, so prosperous. She alone didn't belong. But her shyness had been taken for aloofness, her insecurity for snobbery.

She took a deep breath and looked around the shabby room. She could be as good a neighbor as anybody, she thought with spirit. She would return the friendship the three women had offered. And slowly, as she got to know them better, she would try as hard as she could to explain her feelings about Christmas. They were kind women. They would understand.

IT WAS SATURDAY AFTERNOON, and instead of ripping up carpet, Hedy made divinity. Her mother had taught her how to make the white candy so that it was both rich and light, melting delectably in the mouth. She would take a batch to each of her newly met neighbors.

She was dropping spoonfuls onto a buttered cookie sheet when she heard a commotion coming from Ty's yard. She had noticed children bounding in and out of the house all morning, a few of the limitless number of nieces and nephews, no doubt. Now they were shrieking and yelling in consternation.

A lively confusion around the Marek house on weekends was nothing new. But what the children seemed to be crying out was distinctly peculiar. Hedy looked out the kitchen window. Snow had fallen during the night, and three children stood around Ty's back door, wearing snow boots, jackets, mufflers, and knitted hats. She could have sworn they were all howling something about "Mr. Sneezle."

"He's gone!"

"Mr. Sneezle!"

"—escaped! Runned off!"

"—Mr. Sneezle!"

"—That lady's house!"

"—Mr. Sneeeeeeeee-zle!"

She saw Ty come bolting out of his house, pulling on his green parka. He loped across his yard, vaulted the hedge like an athlete, and then she heard his footsteps on her back porch.

"Mr. Sneeeeeeeeeee-zle!" wailed a niece, her voice rising an impressive number of octaves as she did so.

Ty banged on her back door imperiously. "Quiet!" She heard him command the children.

Hedy set down her mixing bowl and wiped a strand of hair back from her eyes. She swung open the door. She looked up at him suspiciously.

"Mr. Sneeeee-zle!" squalled the niece. "He's losted!"

"What now?" Hedy demanded, pushing her hair back again.

Ty looked harried but determined. "Emergency," he muttered, shouldering past her. "No time to explain." He was across her kitchen in three strides and into her laundry room.

Hedy shut the back door against the cold. She stalked after him. "Why are you bursting in like this?" she asked angrily. "You've got snow all over my floor—"

His height seemed to fill the little room. His hair was tousled and his eyes flashed. He smacked his forehead with the flat of his hand. "Your dryer's open," he said in disgust. He picked up her laundry basket. He began going through her underwear, pausing to make an expert assessment of her brassiere.

"Stop that!" Hedy cried, jerking the laundry basket away from him. "Get your hands off my underwear."

"You don't understand," he growled down at her. He opened the counter under the old sink and stared into its depths.

"Stop that!" Hedy commanded again. She had her hands full with the laundry basket, but she kicked the cabinet door shut.

He rose again, glowering down at her. "It's your fault," he accused. "For leaving the dryer door open."

Hedy, frustrated, stared at the open door of the battered old clothes dryer. For good measure, she kicked it shut, too, but more gently. She was never sure that the dryer wasn't going to fall into a heap of rust.

"My fault?" she asked in disbelief, but he was out of the laundry room and staring intently around the kitchen. "What *is* this?" she demanded again, setting the laundry basket down on the counter.

"You didn't see anything in here?" he demanded. "You've been in here all morning?" He stared significantly at the closed door between the kitchen and dining room. Hedy had shut it to save heat, since she'd been using the kitchen stove. "This door's been shut?"

"Yes," she asserted. "And if you don't tell me—"

He wheeled and headed toward the little back bedroom right off the kitchen. Its door was slightly open. "Ha!" he snarled with the satisfaction of a hunter catching sight of his prey. He strode into her bedroom and, flinging back her bedspread, looked under her bed.

"What are you doing?" Hedy fumed, hot on his heels.

"Mr. Sneezle's lost," Ty grumbled, rising and going to her closet. He began searching through her meager wardrobe. "Have you got a flashlight?"

"Get out of my closet. Who's Mr. Sneezle? What are you doing?"

But he was already out of the closet and pushing past her once again, back into the hall. "Mr. Sneezle escaped from his cage. He got out of the house when one of the kids was going in. They think he jumped into your dryer vent. I saw the tracks. He's in here somewhere."

"Who," Hedy demanded, "is Mr. Sneezle?"

She followed him back into the hall. He opened the door of her linen closet and began rummaging through her small supply of sheets. "Mr. Sneezle the weasel," he said, peering behind a pile of pillowcases.

Hedy tossed her head in a motion that signified that all of her patience had departed and that anything might happen now. "Are you telling me," she said between her teeth, "that there is a weasel loose in my house? A murderous slinking rodent? *Vermin?* Get out of my sheets."

Impatient himself, he turned from the linen closet and looked up and down the hall. "Mr. Sneezle isn't a weasel. Stanley just named him that. To gross out his sisters. Mr. Sneezle's a ferret—a nice, tame ferret. He's so cute that Stanley brought him to visit. Then he escaped. I'll bet he's in the kitchen somewhere—slipped right by you."

Purposefully he strode back to the kitchen. Hedy was right behind him. "Ferret? Ferret?" she said incredulously. "Isn't a ferret just a fancy name for a weasel? Are you telling me there really is a weasel in here? Call an exterminator! Call the police!"

He was rummaging unceremoniously through the cabinets below the counter. "A ferret isn't a weasel," he said impatiently. "It's domesticated, affectionate, a loving pet. It looks a lot like a mink. Think of your house as being lined with mink—somewhere."

"I spent all morning making candy," Hedy warned him. "For gifts. I can't give away food that's had a ferret skipping through it."

He shut the last cabinet door and rose. He glanced at the divinity cooling on the table and then at her.

"You're making candy?" he asked sardonically. "To give away? What's got into you? An ounce of charity? A gram of selflessness?"

"What does it matter, now that some grimy animal's practically tap-danced on it," Hedy flung back.

"He's not grimy," he corrected, his jaw clenching as dangerously as hers. "He's tame, clean, cuddly—and deeply loved by those poor heartbroken little children out there—" he gestured outside, where Hedy could still hear the children fussing.

"All right," Hedy agreed heatedly, although she didn't believe it. "He's clean and cuddly. But he's in *my* house, and now you're pawing through everything I own—"

"Shh!" he said, going suddenly still. He looked out of the corner of his eye at the laundry room again. "Quiet."

"What?" Hedy asked apprehensively. Did he actually see the thing?

"Shh," he repeated in a tone that brooked no disagreement. With a silent, economical movement he took off his parka and hung it over the back of a kitchen chair. Then he started unbuttoning his navy and white flannel shirt. His chest was bare beneath it.

"What—" Hedy gasped.

"I see him," Ty breathed. "He's in the laundry room. He probably never left it."

He slipped out of his shirt. He was standing bare-chested in her kitchen, staring fixedly into the laundry room.

Hedy's brain spun dizzily. His autumn tan had faded, but not completely. She had forgotten the ropes of muscles on his lean arms, the perfectly knit hardness of his chest and back. And she had no idea why he'd removed his shirt. She looked away in embarrassed confusion. "Put your clothes on," she said in a strangled voice.

He ignored her and began to creep silently toward the laundry room. He made a leap at something, throwing his shirt over it. There was a scuffle. "Ha! Got you!" Ty cried triumphantly. He came out of the laundry room with something squirming in his shirt.

His green-brown eyes glittered with victory. He was breathing a bit hard. "No harm done," he said with a satisfied smile. "Want to see him?"

"No!" Hedy objected, taking a step backward.

"Better look," Ty warned, "or in your imagination he'll always be a monster. Come on. I've got him under control."

He peeled back the shirt enough to allow a small, alert face to emerge, along with two neat little paws. The ferret was a beautiful silvery brown, with a charming dark mask like a raccoon's. It had tiny silky ears, bright eyes, and a dainty little pink nose that twitched delicately. It looked almost guilty.

"See?" Ty asked her, admiring the animal. "I think he just came in through the vent and hid behind the dryer. Cute, isn't he?"

Hedy softened as she watched the ferret's curious little face inspecting her kitchen for routes of escape. Ty scratched it behind the ears and cradled it against his bare chest. "Want to pet him?" he asked.

"He won't bite?" she said dubiously.

"I threw the shirt over him to catch him just in case he got excited and tried to bite. But he's fine now. See? He's not a weasel."

Almost mesmerized by the strange and beautiful little creature, Hedy extended a tentative finger. She touched its thick fur, then stroked it. The ferret lowered its inquisitive nose and gave her finger the slightest of ferret caresses. It tickled.

Hedy bit her lip to keep from smiling.

Ty looked down at her, watching her from under a fallen lock of wavy hair. "It's all right," he murmured.

She looked up at him, feeling her heart beating too quickly again. His brown shoulders gleamed in the kitchen's soft light. "What?" she asked, her voice small.

"It's all right," he repeated, studying her face. "To smile, I mean."

She drew her hand back from the lushness of the ferret's fur. But her blue eyes stayed caught in the gaze of his darker ones. Slowly, she smiled. Just as slowly, he smiled back.

It's happening again, she told herself desperately. He was making her feel things that were both complicated and wonderful. He made her feel that simply being alive was a miracle, and she had never realized it until she was with him.

"I'm sorry I got into your underwear," he said huskily, "in the laundry, I mean."

"It's all right," Hedy told him, finding it hard to breathe.

He seemed to be having equal difficulty. "And sorry I got into your bedroom."

"It's all right." She bit her lip again.

His attention focused on her lips. "And sorry I got into your sheets."

"It's all right."

"And if I wasn't holding this blasted ferret..." he murmured, stepping closer to her. He left the sentence unfinished, as his gaze left her mouth and rested on her eyes. The intensity of his stare gave her a fluttery feeling.

"It's all right," Hedy answered softly. She wasn't quite sure what she meant. She was conscious only of his nearness, the breadth of his shoulders and the bare expanse of his chest. He moved closer. He began to lower his head and she began to lift her face to meet his.

Suddenly, somebody was pounding at the back door. They both turned guiltily to face it.

"Uncle Ty!" a boy's voice demanded. "Did you find him?" The question was followed by more insistent pounding. "Uncle Ty? Uncle Ty? Hey!"

Ty glared briefly at the door, then looked down at the ferret resting in his arms. He gave Hedy a wry glance. "Sometimes I get really tired of being 'Uncle Ty.'" He turned back to the door. "Stanley! Stop pounding! I've got him. I'll be right there. Go back to the house."

"He's got him, he's got him, he's got him," Hedy heard the jubilant Stanley announcing as he bounced down the back stairs.

Hedy, her sanity returning, stepped away from Ty's bedazzling nearness. "I'll wrap up some candy for you and the kids," she said, "just to show there're no hard feelings." It wouldn't hurt, she thought, to show him she could be forgiving and generous when she chose.

For once he said nothing at all. He simply stood and watched her as she washed her hands, then set a quantity of the cooled candy on a plate and covered it with foil. She thrust it at him. He took it with his free hand.

He looked her up and down. "Thanks," he said at last. He walked toward the back door and she opened it for him. He stepped past her onto the snow-dusted porch.

The children started squealing as soon as they saw him.

"Your coat," Hedy said, looking after him. He paused at the stairs and threw her another of his long, significant looks. He was still bare-chested in the gray November air. His breath rose in silvery flight. In one arm he had the bright-eyed ferret trapped, peering from the folds of his plaid shirt. In the other he held Hedy's plate. "I'll be back for it," he said, looking into her eyes. "When the kids are gone."

He sauntered down the steps and made his way to a gap in the hedge. As he stepped through, he threw her a parting glance. He smiled.

Hedy closed the door, feeling dizzy again. What she was feeling couldn't be love, she told herself numbly, even if it did have all the usual symptoms. It was impossible that, without knowing it and without wanting it, she had fallen in love with Ty Marek.

But if she hadn't fallen in love with him, she wondered, why was she going to remember him for the rest of her life, just that way: standing bare-chested in the snow, a lock of hair falling over his forehead. Smiling at her.

CHAPTER SEVEN

HEDY TRIED TO GAIN CONTROL of her wayward thoughts and emotions. She had no business entertaining illusions about Ty. She didn't want to speculate about his coming back when the children were gone. She had almost let him kiss her—he *would* have kissed her if Stanley hadn't pounded on the door.

She thanked heaven for Stanley and got ready to deliver her gifts of candy. Her clothing choices were limited: one good winter skirt, black, and one presentable sweater, scarlet. She tugged on her snow boots because the sidewalks looked slippery and put on her red and black jacket and black wool gloves.

She studied herself in the mirror. Although she didn't look stylish like Jolene, she at least looked presentable. She squared her shoulders and started on her rounds.

Emma Gold seemed truly delighted to see her, expressed exuberant appreciation of the candy, and made her sit down and have a cup of coffee. Hedy spent a cozy half hour with her.

"This is a nice neighborhood, you'll like it," Emma Gold assured Hedy as she prepared to take her leave. "I mean nice because the people are kind. They're there when you need them. And you've got the best neighbor of all, the Marek man. Listen, he pretends he's the wild bachelor, but a better man you'll never find. Believe me. I love him like my own. So he's a little crazy? He keeps things lively."

Hedy nodded self-consciously. She wanted to believe Emma Gold's estimation of Ty. Maybe Jolene had exaggerated his womanizing. Maybe Ty himself, wary of commitments, had even exaggerated it a bit.

"I don't know why he hasn't found a wife," Emma said with a frown. "Sometimes I think maybe he's carrying a torch. You know, that there's somebody he can't forget."

Hedy's fragile hopes crashed down around her. She remembered Jolene saying that Ty had never gotten over her. It was very likely he hadn't. She forced herself to smile anyway. "He's very nice," she murmured, not knowing if she was lying or not. What kind of man was Ty Marek, deep down? She didn't know.

"Ignore me," Emma commanded. "What business have I got gossiping about my friend? Excuse me. It's just I see you, I see him, I think—never mind what I think. Button up and stay warm, dear. Come back soon. Don't be a stranger."

Hedy went to Peg Melrose's slightly uproarious household next. The house itself was beautiful, one of the largest on the block. The inside was just as lovely, and kept in order primarily by the force of Peg Melrose's character.

"You—Kenneth," Peg ordered one child as she poured Hedy a cup of coffee. "The hamster does *not* go into the refrigerator. Put him back in his cage, Kenneth. *Now.* Cream and sugar, Hedy?"

Hedy watched in amazement as a child carrying a hamster zoomed through the living room.

Peg Melrose sighed. "Excuse me. I yell like a drill sergeant, but it's a question of who's going to be in charge. I suppose you're used to it, living next door to Ty. He has a real tribe over there sometimes. I'm glad somebody nice bought W.A.'s house. And is fixing it up. We all thought it'd be torn down."

Hedy's cup paused, halfway to her lips. "Torn down?" she said, startled.

Peg nodded, not noticing Hedy's dismay. "The place was so rundown," she sighed. "It was the first house built on this block. And W.A.... .well, he was a love, but he just couldn't manage it those last years. We thought somebody would buy it for the lot, tear it down and build a new one. My husband said he thought the house'd be worth more as salvage. You're brave to take it on. Especially alone. Nobody ever expected a woman would try to fix it up, all by herself."

Peg's frank comments shook Hedy. The house was worth more torn down than standing? Surely that couldn't be right. She tried to act unconcerned. "It'd be easier if I were a master carpenter," she admitted wryly. "If I had it to do over again, I'm not sure I'd take the plunge."

"Well," Peg said, rising to set a fallen toddler back on his feet, "I'm glad you did. I'd hate to see W.A.'s house gone. He was a heck of a man. He started the tradition of decorating the street. It was the year after his wife and daughter died. Both killed in an accident."

Peg sat down again and picked up her coffee cup. "Most people would have climbed into a shell and never come out. But W.A. got up there on his roof and started hanging lights like the neighborhood had never seen. 'Bea and Irene always loved the Christmas lights,' he said. 'I'm doing this for them.' What an attitude. All alone, but he made that house dazzle. Then, one by one, the neighbors caught the spirit, and over the years it became a tradition."

"Yes," Hedy said softly, setting down her cup. "Well, I have a little problem with Christmas myself. You see—"

"Lisa Jo!" Peg cried, rising from her chair, "don't you dare give the baby that chocolate bar! Put it back this *instant*. No candy between meals—you know the rules." She sat back down and grinned. "Sorry, Hedy. But it's the four of them against me. You were saying?"

Hedy looked around at the cheerful room, heard the lively sounds of the children echoing through the house. There was laughter, the sound of running feet, the barking of the poodle. Suddenly she knew she couldn't talk to Peg Melrose about her problems with Christmas. This wasn't the time or place.

"Nothing," Hedy murmured with a shrug. "You were telling me about W.A."

Peg tilted her head and smiled at the memory of him. "Quite an old boy, W.A. Independent as they come. As he got older, he never wanted to admit he could use help keeping that big house up. Ty was the only one slick enough to help him out without him catching on. Ty's one in a million. You ought to grab him."

"What?" Hedy asked, startled again. Her eyes widened.

Peg Melrose grinned mischievously. "Well, *somebody* should grab him," she stated. "I've been trying to get him married off ever since he moved here six years ago. No luck so far."

Hedy could think of nothing to say, but Peg continued cheerfully. "I believe in marriage. But Ty swears he doesn't. I personally think somebody must have really put him through it once. Maybe he still loves her. Who knows? Stranger things have happened."

Hedy nodded uneasily. There it was again. The rumor that Ty had loved someone, lost her, and never gotten over her. And Hedy knew who that someone was: her own incomparable cousin.

"I shouldn't talk about him," Peg said with resignation. "I like him too much. It's just that—well, I can't think of any other reason for a man like him to stay single. But as I said, I shouldn't talk about him. So I won't. Lisa Jo, what did I just tell you about that chocolate bar? Put it *back*, young lady!"

When Hedy at last insisted she must be on her way, Peg shook her hand warmly. "Come back again," she smiled, all her freckles dancing, "if you can stand the uproar. It's so good to talk to an adult—and I like you."

Hedy left the noisy house feeling slightly addled. Peg was as forceful as a small red-haired tornado, and she said exactly what she thought, but it was impossible to dislike her. Hedy mused over what Peg had said. Did he, as Jolene had claimed, still love her, even though she was married? It was a disturbing thought.

Marilyn Hong's house was like a peaceful island of quiet after the boisterousness of the Melrose home. Hedy tried to refuse Marilyn's offer of tea, but at last agreed to stay and have a cup.

"It's nice to talk to someone besides students," Marilyn stated, smiling almost to herself. "I'm fond of them—but after trying to control more than a hundred teenagers all week long, and make them understand algebra, I need contact with the real world."

Hedy smiled in agreement. She, too, spent most of the week caught up in her private interests. It was good to reach out, even casually, to another human being.

"It's shameful," Marilyn Hong said, "that I didn't call on you earlier. We get so caught up in our own affairs."

"I'm as guilty as anyone," Hedy confessed. "I should have made an effort myself. But I felt shy, I guess."

"Shy? Why should a pretty young woman like you ever feel shy?" asked Marilyn, handing Hedy a teacup. She smiled again.

For some reason Hedy felt most at home with this woman, who was superficially the most different from her. "I was afraid I wouldn't fit in," she told her. She looked around at Marilyn's fine things, the velvet sofa, the lacquered coffee table trimmed in brass, the beautiful Chinese vases on the mantel. "Everyone else here seems so—established."

Marilyn poured the tea. Then she leaned back in her chair. She looked like an empress with her crown of blue-black hair. "Everyone fits in on Holly Street," she said. "That's what's special about it. And this season. We celebrate a spirit of tolerance and friendship. I would live nowhere else."

Hedy picked up her teacup. "Yes," she said softly. Here in the welcoming quiet of Marilyn Hong's home, it didn't seem right to disagree. Once again her problems with Christmas seemed out of place, jarring, something best left unspoken. She wanted to talk about it. But she couldn't.

"You'll see," Marilyn told her, watching her face carefully. "Ty Marek says you bought Mr. Tidwell's house to renovate and sell. But maybe after you've lived here a while, you won't want to leave."

Hedy raised her shoulder in a gesture of helplessness. "It's not a question of wanting to leave," she said. "I have to. The house is an investment. That's the only way I can look at it."

"You can't also look upon it as a home?" asked Marilyn, raising an eyebrow gently. "That's unfortunate."

She's right, Hedy thought, struck by the insight. She had never thought of the house as a home, only as a stubborn object she was trying to bend to her will.

There was a greater difference than just money and furnishings between her house and the ones she had visited today. The houses of Emma Gold, Peg Melrose, and Marilyn Hong were homes. They were loved.

She searched for the right words. "Sometimes," she admitted, "I think I try too hard—I don't take any time off from worrying about it. It seems as if I'm carrying the weight of the whole house on my back."

"Perhaps you need a lesson from your neighbor," suggested Marilyn, sipping her tea. "From Ty Marek. He's a most remarkable man, you know."

"I know," murmured Hedy. She gazed down at the carpet.

"You may think he is lazy and superficial. Don't be fooled. He tries to mislead people, but I know him too well. He isn't what he pretends to be."

Hedy no longer thought Ty either lazy or superficial, but she was eager to hear Marilyn Hong's opinion. "How?" she asked.

"He works very hard," Marilyn said. "Only with a writer, like a mathematician, the work is mostly up here." She tapped her forehead with one slim finger. "One of my nephews is a journalist in San Francisco. He says Ty amazes him. He asks how one man can consistently produce work of such high quality, and as often as he does. Yes, he's always thinking, Ty Marek. And feeling, as well."

"Feeling?"

"If anything, he feels too much. Which is why he tries to disguise the fact that he feels at all."

Hedy shook her head. "If he has any emotions other than a passion for his hammock, he keeps them well hidden," she said ruefully.

"The two of you are alike in some ways. You keep many things locked up inside." Marilyn studied her over the rim of her teacup. "Well, things that get locked up have a way of escaping sometimes. Like the—ferret? Is that what that creature was this morning?"

Hedy looked aghast. Marilyn laughed.

"I was hanging new curtains this morning," Marilyn explained. "I heard the children cry out. I looked and saw the thing streak across the snow and dive into the vent. Then Ty leaping from his house. Did he find it? I stopped peeking. It seemed wrong."

"He found it," Hedy almost whispered, embarrassed. She remembered all too clearly Ty standing in her kitchen, his moving toward her, bending to her, almost kissing her.

"Yes," Marilyn repeated crisply. "Well, I mention the creature only to make a point. Locked-up things do escape. It's their nature to try."

Hedy smiled hesitantly. "The point? I'm not sure I see it."

"The point," Marilyn Hong said, "is that the two of you are people who try to keep your emotions imprisoned. But emotions get out, one way or another. It's best to let them go sometimes. To be honest about them."

"It's not always easy to be honest," Hedy answered, knowing Marilyn had guessed her secret feelings for Ty. "It's not even possible. Things get complicated. They get all tied up with the past...and other things," she ended lamely.

"There's an old saying about the past," Marilyn observed, looking at her kindly. "Those who don't understand the past are doomed to repeat it."

"I'm not quite sure what you mean," Hedy returned, puzzlement in her face.

"I mean, Hedy, do you really understand the past? In all honesty? Do you and Ty understand the same things about it?"

Hedy was silent a moment. "I'm not sure," she said at last. "Our relationship has been rocky. For some reason there's been very little understanding, really. Of the past—or anything else."

"Then perhaps you should talk, the two of you."

Hedy shook her head again. "I don't know that we can."

"One of you should try, I think," Marilyn suggested. "I realize I'm meddling. You haven't asked for my opinion or advice. But I can tell that you're disturbed. And Ty's own emotions are unruly. Why else would he donate that five hundred dollars in your name?"

"What?" Hedy asked, astonished. "You know?"

"I guessed," Marilyn smiled. "Don't worry, I've said nothing to the others. Ty may fool them. Me, he can't fool."

Hedy gazed at her in wonder. "How did you know?"

"Hedy," she replied, smiling, "if I were easily fooled, I couldn't cope with students. I teach them math. They teach me about human behavior. Ty's story was—how can I put it?—a little too pat. And your reaction was too genuine. But I didn't feel it my place to embarrass you any further in front of the others."

Hedy laughed in mortification. "I feel silly, thinking I'd kept the truth from you."

Marilyn leaned over and patted her hand. "Let people believe what Ty wants for the time being. Whatever else he thinks he accomplished by this trick, one thing is sure. We've met and we'll be friends, I think."

"I think you're right," Hedy said with a smile.

When she walked the short distance back to her house, her heart felt curiously light, and she was warm all over in spite of the cold. She had come to know three fine neighbors today. Better yet, one of them, Marilyn, was going to be special.

For the first time when Hedy walked into her house, she felt she had come home. She went to the kitchen window and looked at Ty's house, brilliant orange against the snow. "She's right," Hedy whispered, as if he could hear her. "We should be honest with each other. We could find out about the past. And how much the past really matters."

She turned and looked at the kitchen table. The light from outside was fading swiftly. Draped over a chair was Ty's green parka. He would be coming back. Soon.

HEDY WAS RESTLESS. She didn't change back into her work clothes. She drifted through the house aimlessly. Slowly the presence of W.A. Tidwell was fading away. Bit by bit, the house was becoming hers.

And, she noted wryly, it hadn't fallen down because she'd neglected it for a day. *A whole day,* she thought, marveling. She'd wasted a whole day, not working, not studying.

No, she corrected, she hadn't wasted it; she had spent it getting to know her neighbors. Perhaps, just perhaps, she might get to know Ty, the most distracting, mysterious, and troubling of all possible neighbors, better, too.

She moved through the living room, noticing how unlived-in it looked. Security slept on the sofa, inert as a large furry pillow. Hedy reached down and petted her. The cat, as usual, did not respond.

"Of all the cats in the world," Hedy said, shaking her head, "I picked you. Which just proves looks aren't everything."

When the telephone rang, it startled her so much she jumped. She glanced at her watch. It was almost eight o'clock. She wondered who would phone her on a Saturday night.

Hedy hurried to answer the phone's persistent jangle.

"Hedy?" It was Jolene's velvety voice. "It's me. Listen, it's an emergency. I need your help."

An emergency, Hedy thought, all her familial feelings rallying. "Of course."

"I'm sorry I haven't been in touch, been helping you more," Jolene said quickly, "but I've been having a devil of a time. It's Melvin. He's jealous. Of everything, including my career. He wants me to give it up. I—well, I'm thinking about leaving him."

"Jolene, no," Hedy said, aghast. Jolene had been married to Melvin for six years. Although Hedy had never met him, she thought the two of them were perfectly happy together.

"I've called Ty," Jolene went on, almost breathlessly. "He's always really loved me. He's always understood me. I'm meeting him tonight. At the Mayfair. If my parents should try to find me through you, don't tell them where I am. Or Melvin, if he calls you."

Hedy felt her heart take a long, sickening dive. She felt it land on stone. "Ty?" she asked helplessly.

"Yes," Jolene answered in a dramatic whisper. "Maybe. Oh, Hedy, I'm so confused. Melvin just has me so upset—I don't know what to do, I really don't."

There was a beat of silence. "Why are you telling me this?" Hedy asked at last. She knew the question sounded cold, but she felt cold, frozen to the bone.

"In case my parents need to get a message to me for any reason," Jolene answered. "I mean, if Melvin calls them, they're going to be very, very upset. If they call, tell them I'm fine, I'm in good hands, but don't tell them where I am. Melvin can always twist Mother around his little finger."

"I see," Hedy said tonelessly.

"So just tell anyone who asks that I'm fine," Jolene insisted. She made a sound like a small, feminine growl. "Oh, that Melvin! I'll make him see things my way. Or I'll walk right out on him. There are other fish in the sea."

Yes, thought Hedy numbly, *and some of them are sharks.*

"Okay," Jolene told her. "Our little secret, all right? You're a darling, Hedy. Talk to you later."

With a click, the line went dead. Hedy set down the receiver. She felt hollow. She felt foolish and betrayed. She sat down, unseeing, on the sofa.

She should have taken Jolene's warning from the beginning. She should have seen Ty for what he was. Hedy was the foolish little country mouse from Fox Creek, and she had blundered into a situation far too sophisticated for her to understand. Ty had amused himself with her. But now he would have no more need to.

She heard footsteps on her front porch. There was a knock. It sounded confident, even jaunty, echoing through the big house.

Ty Marek.

What did he want with her? She got up, back very straight, and went to the kitchen.

As she picked up his parka, the cloth seemed to sear her fingers. She went to the front door and pulled it open.

He stood there, leaning against the frame, smiling down at her. "I thought those kids'd never go," he said, looking deep into her eyes. "And now I found out I can't stay. A kind of emergency's come up. But, Hedy, when it's over, we need to talk. We'll need to talk a long time. I know it's hard to understand. I'm not the kind of guy who makes commitments, but I can only promise you—"

"Don't promise me anything," Hedy retorted coldly. She thrust the coat at him. "I don't have anything to say to you. I don't give a damn about your commitments or lack of them. I have a future to build. I don't have time for your games."

First amazement, then disbelief, then anger crossed his face. He stared down at her, clutching his coat. "Look, what's got into you? Grow up, will you? I only—"

She slammed the door. She ignored it when he knocked again. She ignored it when he called her name in a low, angry voice.

"I hate you," she whispered fiercely at his departing footsteps. She said it with all the conviction in her soul. He wasn't sure yet that he had his beloved Jolene, so he would try to make sure Hedy was there to comfort him if he failed. "I hate you," she repeated.

She sat alone, her hands clenched in her lap. *How ironic,* she thought, looking at the scarred, bare walls. A few brief hours before, this grim old house had almost felt like home. It didn't now. She doubted that it ever would again.

CHAPTER EIGHT

TY WAS GONE ALL THAT NIGHT and the next three nights, as well. Various relatives came and went, looking after the dog and cat. Then, just as inexplicably, he was home again, and trying to call her. Hedy hung up when she heard his voice.

Jolene phoned with the cryptic news that she and Melvin had reached a partial understanding. She was home again.

So that was it, Hedy thought darkly. Jolene had once again rejected Ty, so he was up to his old tricks.

He tried to confront her on Thursday night when she came home from her night class. She shouldered her way past him, ignoring him.

"Hedy," he demanded, reaching out and seizing her arm, "listen to me. I know what's wrong."

She pulled away from him roughly. She ran up the stairs and unlocked her door before he could say another word. After slamming it shut behind her, she leaned against it, breathing hard, as if she had escaped something that menaced her life.

Next, he left a letter in a long white envelope sticking out of her mailbox. It had her first name scrawled on it in his distinctive wide-swinging handwriting. She plucked it out as if it were a dead rodent, crumpled it into a wad and hurled it into a bank of freshly fallen snow. *Let his words freeze all winter and smear into the mud in the spring,* she thought.

For three more days he tried to make contact with her. Then he quit trying.

He was probably off chasing the Canarsi twins, Hedy thought grimly. Or the firmly muscled Myra Rubicoff. Or any of the innumerable other available women in Chicago.

She felt more homesick than ever for Tippy and her family. There were no dark secrets or intrigue or elaborate games in Tippy's house or Tippy's heart. Tip's existence might be precarious sometimes, but it was better than the complicated melodrama of Jolene and Melvin and Ty.

Hedy tried to regain her bearings by inviting herself to Marilyn Hong's for tea. But there was little she could say to Marilyn without revealing family secrets that best remained hidden. The affair, Hedy thought dryly, was Jolene's after all.

"You and Ty," Marilyn said, pouring from the ornately decorated teapot, "you never had your talk? Forgive me. I don't spy on you. You look unhappy, that's all."

Hedy wriggled her toes in her boots. She wondered once more why she should feel so at home in Marilyn's beautiful house. "I don't think we *can* talk," she admitted pessimistically. "It's an unpleasant situation. And nobody should think of Ty and me as a pair. There's—there's another woman."

Another woman, Hedy thought darkly. What a dreaded, dreadful, and overly dramatic phrase. "There has been for some time," she said, so it didn't sound quite as theatrical. "Somebody he's known for a long while."

"Oh," said Marilyn. "I see."

"I mean," Hedy said philosophically, "people have suspected, haven't they? Both Emma Gold and Peg Melrose said as much. That Ty had—had a thing about some woman that he couldn't get over."

Marilyn raised one fine, dark eyebrow. "There's that rumor, yes. It's quite romantic, I suppose. To think he's brooding over some great love."

And settling for any number of small loves when he couldn't possess the great one, Hedy thought bitterly.

"As rumors go, it's a good one," Marilyn continued when Hedy said nothing. "But I never believed it. Do you know why?"

"No."

"Because he doesn't act like a man with a broken heart. He acts like a man whose heart was broken, but healed. Too well, perhaps. Or the wrong way. Too much scar tissue. If we are to indulge in the genteel pastime of guessing our neighbor's secrets, that's my contribution."

Hedy shrugged and tried to smile. She couldn't tell Marilyn about her painful conversation with Jolene. She didn't know if she ever wanted to tell anyone about it.

Marilyn saw that she was troubled and changed the subject. "We have to go through the Christmas ornaments this weekend. Soon all the decorations go up. Every year my husband and I wonder why we get caught up in all this fuss. And every year we decide again that it's worth it. You'll be surprised at how many people come to see the lights of Holly Street."

Hedy stared into her teacup. "I don't know if I can do it," she said softly. She didn't want to look at Marilyn.

"Hedy!" Marilyn said, leaning forward in her chair. "You don't think you can do what? You look so sad. Is something wrong?"

Marilyn's face was so kind and gentle, yet strong, that Hedy found herself haltingly explaining the trouble she had with Christmas: the hard year on the tree farm, her father's first heart attack coming at Christmas, her mother's final stroke coming at exactly the same time five years later. It was hard to make the words come, but with Marilyn's understanding, she finally forced the whole story out.

"I didn't know when I bought the house," Hedy finished shakily, "that everyone was expected to celebrate Christmas in a big way. I'm not sure I'm up to it. Not yet."

Marilyn exhaled softly. "Ah, Hedy, Hedy, I'm sorry. This is why Ty Marek put all that money in the Christmas fund for you? You would not? Or could not?"

Hedy nodded. "Both. I couldn't face it. I wouldn't."

Marilyn was silent a long moment. "Then you won't have to," she said at last. "I'll explain to the others. Don't participate, Hedy. Not if it causes you pain. The people here are kind. They'll understand."

"Oh, Marilyn," Hedy said, gratitude knotting her throat. "Thank you. I mean it. You don't have to tell them all the details—in fact, I'd rather you didn't—just that there's a general problem. I don't know how I can thank you enough."

"You don't?" Marilyn sounded cheerful surprised. "I do."

"How?"

"I'm having a get-together Friday night. I have no dinner partner for my nephew Alex. He's a nice young man, most personable, really. Would you do me the honor?"

Hedy hesitated, slightly bewildered. She had nothing to wear to a party in a house as fine as this.

Marilyn gave a delicate little cough. "Of course, I'd understand if you have other engagements."

Oh, heavens, Hedy thought. Did Marilyn think she was prejudiced and wouldn't want to have dinner with her nephew?

"I'd love to come," she stated earnestly. "I was just brooding about what to wear. That's all."

"Wear your black skirt and red sweater," Marilyn said. "You'll look fine. Just fine."

When Hedy left Marilyn's house, she felt almost buoyant. Perhaps there was life after Ty Marek after all. And

Marilyn had understood Hedy's confused emotions about Christmas and would see that she was spared celebrating it. She was a kind friend, and a good and wise one.

Snow was starting to fall again. Hedy entered her house with rosy cheeks and a tingling nose. She turned up the old heater. Sometimes it overwarmed the room, and sometimes it had a mysterious chilly spell. Today it was having one of its fits of stinginess, and no matter how high Hedy turned it, the room stayed cold.

Security waddled by her, nose in the air. She leaped up on the seat of a dining-room chair, trying to find the most cushiony spot she could near the heater. The cat was getting fat, Hedy noted absently. She'd have to cut down on its food.

A horrible thought crossed her mind. What if Security was going to have kittens? And those kittens were fathered by that villainous-looking cat that belonged to Ty Marek?

No, Hedy thought. She refused even to contemplate it. She was becoming expert at avoiding unpleasant thoughts. There had been so many lately on which to practice.

WINTER CLAMPED DOWN on Chicago. Snow had started early and fell with depressing regularity. The yards on Holly Street were heaped with it, and the street itself always seemed to be garbed in a dirty cloak of slush.

The temperature had plummeted in early November and refused to rise. Chicago's fabled winds took on a cutting edge, and weathermen kept talking about the dismal "windchill factor," and how, the stronger the gales grew, the lower they made the temperature feel.

The old house shook and creaked in the wind. The heater didn't begin to keep the place warm, and Hedy stayed bundled up as she worked. She had stained the woodwork and started hanging the paper downstairs. The job seemed triply hard when she worked with numbed fingers.

The only positive result of the cold was that Security's winter coat grew long, lush, and lovely. The cat resembled a huge smoke-gray puffball. She grew rounder every day, and Hedy hoped it was the luxuriant winter pelt, and not unwanted kittens. The last thing Hedy needed was kittens to remind her of Ty Marek.

She worked as hard at not thinking of Ty as she did at restoring the house. Marilyn Hong tried to help her, as tactfully as possible. She invited Hedy over for tea often, and introduced her to still more neighbors.

The party that Marilyn gave had been friendly and comfortable. Marilyn's nephew Alex was all any woman might hope for. He was tall, he was dark, he was handsome, he was polite, he was intelligent, he was charming. He had asked Hedy out and she had gone with him.

He took her on a tour of Chicago's Chinatown, its Little Italy section, and its Greek neighborhood. She had never eaten so much or sampled so many kinds of wonderful food. Alex had even teased her into trying fried squid, which she was amazed to discover was delicious.

They tarried briefly in the Art institute and Hedy marveled at the museum's collection of famous paintings. He showed her a dazzling display of the city's riches: the startling beauty of Daley Plaza, the vitality of State Street, and the greatest jewels in Chicago's wealth of fabled architecture.

He had asked her out a second time, an invitation to the theater, and Hedy had accepted. Alex was a comfortable, courteous, and pleasant companion. He was so tall and handsome that Hedy caught other women stealing envious glances at him. He was a professor of computer sciences, and shrewd investments had made him a moderately wealthy man.

No woman could ask for more, Hedy told herself, amazed that he showed the slightest interest in her. But when he asked her for a third date, she was surprised to find herself refusing. Some chemistry was lacking between them. Even when she was enjoying herself most with Alex, she found herself thinking longingly of Ty Marek. Alex seemed to understand. He didn't press her.

Why her thoughts kept returning to Ty, Hedy didn't know. The phenomenon disgusted her. Repeatedly she enumerated his faults with a sort of perverse pleasure. He was adulterous, self-indulgent, lecherous, manipulative, and unprincipled. She hated him, she told herself.

But every time she thought of his lopsided grin and green-brown eyes, she felt such a pang in her heart that she could clearly imagine it, like a cartoon heart, broken in to two jagged halves. She seldom caught sight of him these days, for which she was thankful.

Then, one night when November was ending, she met him again under the worst circumstances. The weather had been so horrible that Hedy suspected it was showing off, letting people know just how tough, nasty and bullying Chicago weather could be.

Snow mixed with frigid rain had fallen for a night and half a day. Then the temperature tumbled to below zero and the winds rose, shrieking like banshees. Snow began in earnest, an endless storm of stinging, ice-cold needles.

Even Chicagoans, who usually took any weather in their stride, were dismayed. Streets were impossible to navigate. The state police warned people to stay off the highways, and downtown Chicago was said to be paralyzed, with people stranded in stores and office buildings.

Hedy's night class was canceled. She stayed home, grateful for the erratic warmth sputtering from the old heater. It was at precisely five o'clock in the evening, when the sky was already black, that Hedy discovered Security was having kittens. Or, at least, the cat was trying to, but something was wrong.

Hedy had discovered Security hiding in the laundry room, lying in the clothes basket and panting. "Oh, no," she said, almost sick with anger. This could only mean that Ty's hideous cat was about to become a father. What would she do with the afflicted offspring, who would doubtlessly be as ugly as Benchley, with his mud-colored coat and crazed eyes?

But before much time passed, Hedy realized that the cat's trouble was serious. The kittens were trying to be born, but nature wasn't cooperating. Hedy, overcome by concern, forgot her anger. What should she do? What *could* she do?

She stared helplessly at the quietly suffering cat. Cats weren't supposed to have such problems. Cats were supposed to produce kittens as effortlessly as trees produced leaves. The barn cat back in Michigan made kittens appear with such apparent ease that Hedy's mother had joked that the cat didn't really have the kittens, it got them by mail order every few months. But Security, obviously, was different.

Hedy could not stand to see a creature in pain. When anything suffered, Hedy suffered with it and intensely. Now she felt sick with distress for the cat and helpless, as well.

Finally it occurred to her to call a veterinarian—if any were answering. She might not be able to get the cat to the vet, but at least he could tell her what to do.

Her hands trembling, she looked in the telephone book. She lifted the receiver, then started to dial. She stopped. There was no dial tone. The phone was dead.

Gritting her teeth in frustration, she hung up. She stared at the cat. She had brought the basket in by the heater. Security, who had always seemed so aloof and without concern for anything, was now locked bravely in her own private battle. She made no sound of pain or fear.

Maybe her phone was the only one out, Hedy thought desperately. The wires leading to the house were old, and so covered with ice, they might have broken in the wind. She would go to Marilyn's and try to call from there.

She bundled herself into her jacket, boots, muffler and gloves. The wind struck her as forcefully as a malicious blow when she opened the door.

She could barely see, and the porch was slippery with ice under a treacherous blanket of snow. She descended the stairs and, keeping her head down, tried to make her way toward Marilyn's house. The wind turned her halfway around, and she was almost dizzied by it. She was already losing her sense of direction.

She hurtled into something tall and hard. "Oof!" she gasped. She reached out instinctively for support.

Gloved hands reached back, grasping her arms. She felt something protecting her from the full force of the wind as strong arms turned her away from its harshest impact. She blinked up through the stinging darkness.

Ty stood there, squinting back at her. His body shielded hers from the wind, and he pulled her closer to him, as if to protect her even more. His hands gripped her arms tightly, but she was already so cold she could barely feel his touch.

"What are you doing out here?" he demanded, the wind whipping his thick hair. "Are you crazy?"

For a long second she was too stunned by his sudden appearance and his nearness to respond. Then everything, including how eager Ty had been to undermine Melvin and Jolene's marriage, came rushing back to her.

"I have to get to a phone. That stupid cat of yours, that—that gruesome monster—has my poor cat in trouble. She's trying to have kittens but she can't—and my phone's dead. Now let go of me."

She tried to struggle away from him. He held her fast. "Whoa!" he ordered, bending closer to her so that the wind didn't tear away his words. "Where do you think you're going?"

"Marilyn's," Hedy said, trying to shake off his hands. Once again she was unsuccessful. He kept her in his grip.

"Don't bother," he ordered. "There aren't any lights on there. She probably went home with somebody who lives closer to school. Sam probably can't get home from downtown. I hear even the computer trains are having trouble."

Hedy strained her eyes against the wind and the snow. He was right. Marilyn's lights were off. So were the Golds'. At the very end of the street, lights blazed in the Melrose house, but the cold made them seem endless miles away.

"Come on," he said roughly, nodding at his house. "Into my place. You can use mine if it's working."

The wind was so strong that Hedy had little choice but to let him wrap one arm around her and lead her up the slippery sidewalk and onto his porch. He kept her in his protective embrace as he unlocked his front door and swung it open. He ushered her inside, practically lifting her over the threshold.

Mrs. Parker, the dog, overcome with emotion, hurled herself at Ty's legs, yipping madly of her love. As Ty switched on the lights, Hedy saw the evil Benchley himself, crouching on the easy chair and staring at her with his slightly insane eyes.

He looked as if he was trying to put a curse on her, Hedy thought darkly, and he seemed to have succeeded. "Men," she growled at him, venom in her voice.

"What?" Ty said, trying to quiet Mrs. Parker. The dog was practically sobbing her appreciation of having her master home. Ty had snow in his hair and snow was thick on the shoulders of his parka and on his tall leather boots.

"Nothing," Hedy muttered. She looked around, suddenly ill at ease. She had never seen the inside of Ty's house. It was surprisingly homey, with a deep twilight-blue carpet and lots of comfortable, tweedy furniture. But, Ty being Ty, there was also an oil painting of Scrooge McDuck over the mantel.

She brushed snow from her sleeve and gave Ty a suspicious look. "What were you doing out there?" she asked. "Don't tell me the Canarsi twins are jogging in this weather."

"I've given up watching the Canarsi twins," he grumbled. "It stopped being fun. I was out there because I drove my car into a ditch. Or rather it drove itself. Damned ice."

"Oh, no," Hedy said, instantly sympathetic in spite of herself. "Why were you even trying to drive?"

"My sister Maria's got a sick kid," he said. "I picked up a prescription for her. I made it all right until I was four blocks from here. Then somebody pulled the road out from under me."

"Are you all right?"

"Only my pride's hurt," he answered, unzipping his parka. He grimaced in distaste. "I thought I could drive that thing through hell itself. Another illusion smashed. Not to mention the front end of the car. Why are you staring at me like that?"

Startled, Hedy pretended to flick a melting snowflake from her glove. "I didn't realize I was staring. Or that it was in any particular way."

He put a fist on his hip. He scrutinized her. "Yeah? For a minute you looked almost as if you gave two cents about what happened to me."

"It must have been a trick of the light," she said, still not looking at him.

He shook his head, his brows drawn together. "You've got a smart mouth, know that? I don't know whether it's what I like best about you—or least. Maybe it's both. Come on. Let's see if the phone is working."

He crossed the room to a blue telephone sitting on a walnut table and picked up the receiver. "My phone works fine," he said with a mocking smile. "I guess God likes me better than you."

"You've got a smart mouth, yourself," Hedy retorted.

He smiled again. "Well, who's smart mouth shall we use to call a vet? Yours or mine?"

"Suit yourself," she muttered, crossing her arms defensively. They were doing it again, bringing out the worst in each other.

"Then let me," he replied with a sardonic bow. "I live to serve." He flopped into a nearby armchair, picked up the telephone book and set the phone itself on his chest. "A vet," he said grimly. "Shouldn't be any harder than finding a square egg. You might as well sit down. This isn't going to be fast, you know."

"I'll stand," Hedy asserted.

Forty-five minutes later she had capitulated. Her coat off, her snow boots off, she curled self-consciously in the chair opposite Ty's. She played anxiously with the fringe on her muffler.

Ty was speaking earnestly into the phone. After trying innumerable vets, he had finally found one who answered. But success seemed short-lived. Ty was talking, but he didn't look happy.

He hung up and got to his feet. "Come on," he said without enthusiasm. "I've got to take her to him. I hope your car starts."

"You don't have to do anything," Hedy said, almost guiltily. "I'll take her. Where is he?"

"The edge of Lombard," he answered, his mouth set in resignation. "And you're not driving anyplace. You're a sissy driver."

"I am not."

"Yes, you are," he said with disdain. "I've seen you. You creep around even when the weather's fine. You—drive in this? That's a laugh."

Hedy slipped into her jacket and pulled on her knitted cap and boots. She knew what he said was true. He was a bold and confident driver, she a timorous one. Chicago's legendary traffic had hardened him to fearlessness, but it reduced her to jelly.

He opened the door for her. Once again the wind struck like an assault. In the minute and a half it took to go from Ty's house to hers, Hedy felt as if she were frozen through.

"Where's the cat?" he asked, his voice joyless.

"Here," she answered, showing him the laundry basket. Poor Security lay stretched out, her mouth open, her eyes glazed.

For once he said nothing uncomplimentary about the cat. He looked at it with concern, even though Hedy could tell he was trying to keep his face stern.

"Give me your keys," he ordered. "I'll get the car warmed up, then I'll come back for her."

"I'll bring her," she said. "I'm going with you."

"No," he returned with implacable firmness, "you're not. It's dangerous out there. We don't both have to take a chance on getting killed because of this—" he glanced down at the unfortunate cat without finishing the sentence. "I won't take you," he concluded. Hedy could tell he meant it. He went out to the driveway.

Ten minutes later he stalked back into the house. He looked angrier than Hedy had ever seen him.

"What's wrong?" she asked, eyeing his stormy expression.

"Your damned car won't start," he growled. "It's frozen solid. Wrap the cat up. I'll carry her."

"You mean walk?" Hedy asked in horror.

"No," he answered sarcastically, "I'll wave my magic wand and fly. Of course, I mean walk. My car's in a ditch, yours won't start, and if anybody else'd be crazy enough to lend me a car, I wouldn't be crazy enough to take a chance on wrecking it. Wrap her up and hand her over."

"Ty," she protested, "you can't. It's below zero out there—"

"You want the cat to die?" he asked bluntly.

"Of course not—"

"Give her here," he ordered.

Hedy put the groggy cat into a towel-lined box of heavy cardboard. She shut the lid, leaving a small opening for fresh air. Then she wrapped a quilt around the box, with only the air hole unprotected.

Ty took the box without comment. He started toward the door.

"Ty," Hedy practically wailed, "you don't even have a muffler. Take mine."

"No," he muttered. "I want to suffer as much as possible. Why be miserable if you can't be completely miserable? Come on, cat, let's take a walk."

As he opened the door, a blast of wind came snarling in. He left, stepping into the storm.

To Hedy, the next hours seemed endless. She envisioned every imaginable hazard that could befall Ty and the cat.

People died in storms like this, she told herself. It happened every winter. At least if Ty made it to the vet's, he could stay there. He would be safe if not comfortable. And he could have the pleasure of claiming that, because of her, he'd been forced to sleep among hospitalized dogs and cats and parakeets while the blizzard raged.

Two and a half hours crawled by. She knew he might be safe but couldn't call because her phone was out. She worried anyway. For the past weeks she had forced herself to dwell on all Ty's flaws. Now that he was gone, disappeared into the cold and the dark and the wind, she thought of all the things she missed about him.

She missed his irreverence, his humor, the intensity concealed beneath his jokes, the quickness of his mind, the warmth he usually tried to hide from her. She realized she even missed arguing with him. Arguing with Ty was more challenging than anything she could think of, with the possible exception of getting along with him.

Another hour dragged by, minute by leaden minute. The wind howled. Hedy worried. The night was worthy of the Arctic Circle.

When she heard a pounding on her door shortly before midnight, she was so astonished she nearly wept with happiness. She ran to open it.

Ty stepped inside. He was covered with snow and he had ice in his eyebrows. His boots were caked with white, and he stamped them gingerly, as if he no longer had feeling in his feet.

"Are you all right?" she gasped. "I shouldn't have let you go. Why did you walk back, for heaven's sake? Why didn't you stay?"

He held up a hand to silence her. He seemed to have to search deep within himself to find his voice. "The cat's fine," he managed to say. He kicked off his boots, peeled off his gloves, and started to shrug out of his coat.

"I'll make coffee," Hedy said, desperate to do something to help. "Oh, I shouldn't have let you go. You shouldn't have come back. You shouldn't."

He took a deep breath. "Not your instant coffee," he ordered, shaking his head. "Something stronger. You've got five healthy kittens." His voice ragged. "Did I say the cat's fine?"

Hedy nodded, then dashed into the kitchen. She had a small bottle of vodka she had bought months ago for Jolene when she visited. She took it from the cabinet and filled a water glass half full. Ty had stalked to the kitchen after her, rubbing his hands together. His face was dark from the cold.

She looked at him, decided he needed more than a mere half tumbler of liquor, and filled the glass to the brim. She held it toward him.

He shook his head. "I'm not sure I can hold it," he said between his teeth.

At first Hedy didn't understand. Then she realized his fingers were so benumbed he couldn't grasp the glass. He would be lucky if he escaped frostbite.

"I can't believe you did this," she said, fighting back tears. She knew the walk must have been terrible. He would probably feel the cold within him for hours. He would probably get sick. He would probably get pneumonia. He would probably die, and it would be her fault.

"Aren't you going to ask about the kittens?" he said, taking another deep breath. He tried to flex his fingers, but the action obviously pained him.

"Are *you* all right?" she demanded, her voice shaking. She watched him clench and unclench the fingers of both hands. At last he picked up the glass. He raised it to his lips and drank half the vodka with one long pull. He exhaled sharply. Then he took another drink.

"Let's see," he rasped. "I said there were five, right?"

Hedy nodded, her teeth chattering in sympathetic cold pangs. Ty's arduous journey had left him slightly disoriented, but he was struggling hard to regain his normal balance.

"Three are gray. Two look like they might have Siamese markings. They don't look so bad. And your cat's fine. She can have other kittens. You won't lose your money. I'll pay the vet's bill." He finished the last of the vodka. "Now," he said, "maybe I could face some of your coffee."

She lit the fire beneath the kettle. "I don't care about the money," she told him, shaking her head in frustration. "And you're not paying for the vet—"

"Yes, I am."

"The money doesn't matter," she insisted. "What matters is you're all right. Why did you walk clear back?"

He took another deep breath. "So you wouldn't worry." He leaned against the edge of the kitchen door and folded his arms. "About the poor cat."

The words "poor cat" touched Hedy's heart. As much as Ty pretended to hate Security, he had actually pitied her enough to walk those long miles in the storm.

A tear spilled onto her cheek and she brushed it away furiously, hoping he hadn't seen. "I can't believe you did this," she repeated, hating all the emotions that surged through her. "You—you took a vow never to walk more than five blocks. Never to exert yourself."

"I can't believe it, either." He looked at her, his face almost solemn.

"Ty, you walked ten miles in this blizzard," she stated in exasperation. "Probably over ten miles. It must have been awful."

She couldn't help it. She was so glad to see him, so grateful for what he had done, that the tears rose in her eyes again. He watched them glitter and said nothing. He just kept leaning against the door, his eyes on hers.

"Well, can't I do anything?" Hedy demanded, afraid that the tears had betrayed her totally. "Besides just give you a cup of coffee that you're going to hate?"

"Yes," he said. He straightened up and took a step toward her, looking down into her eyes.

"What?" She almost whispered the word. Almost without volition she stretched out her arms toward him. She put her hands on either side of his face. It was still icy cold.

He put his arms around her and she did not resist. He lowered his face to hers. "Warm me, Hedy," he breathed.

She did.

CHAPTER NINE

HIS LIPS were at first like ice against hers, then like flame. She kept the warmth of her hands against his face. He pulled her tightly against him, and she tried to press more closely still, to give him all the heat of her body.

"Hedy," he murmured against her lips. "You feel like fire. The good kind. That gives life." He kissed her again.

She was so filled with emotion for him that she almost sobbed against his mouth. He wrapped his arms around her more possessively. His hands, moving across her back, were cold, and she pulled her shirt from her jeans, signaling him to warm himself against the heat of her flesh.

She shivered at first when his hands touched her skin. He inhaled sharply, almost gasped, then kissed her more deeply. Her lips parted and his tongue invaded the warmth of her mouth, exploring hungrily.

"Hedy," he muttered again, burying his face in her hair.

She slid her hands under his heavy sweater, exploring the rippling muscles of his back. His skin was still cold beneath her fingers, but when she touched him, both their bodies turned into flame that gave pleasure but no pain.

He pulled her as close to him as he could. "Hedy," he breathed in her ear, "warm me all over."

She laid her cheek against his broad chest and nodded in assent. He picked her up easily. She kept her eyes closed, her face buried against the wool of his sweater, as if she could shut out the reality of what she was doing as well as its consequences. She heard him turn off the kettle. She felt him bearing her down the little hallway, into the small downstairs bedroom. The room was cold. He did not bother to turn on the light.

He lowered her to the bed and immediately stretched out beside her, pulling her to him once more. "Get under the covers," she whispered. "It's cold." She was still concerned for him.

"I forgot," he whispered back. He pulled the quilts back and covered them both, wrapping her more tightly in his arms, so that they both burrowed into the comfort of the soft old mattress.

For a moment he fumbled with the buttons of her shirt, but his fingers were still too stiff with cold to be agile. He sighed in exasperation and gave up.

Shyly, Hedy unbuttoned her shirt for him. He sighed again, this time with satisfaction. He drew back from her long enough only to shrug out of his heavy sweater. He took her hand and laid it against the front of his flannel shirt. She understood. Slowly, more shyly still, she unbuttoned it, too.

He put his arms around her again and his lips traveled down the smoothness of her throat, until he was kissing the warm valley between her breasts. Then he bent his face to her breasts and kissed them to burning desire.

Hedy ran her fingers through the thick silk of his hair. His body against hers was no longer cold, but fervid with the vibrant heat of passion. It seemed as if he could not touch her enough.

The air around them was crisp and cool. Once, when he moved to shape his body more closely to hers, the quilts slid away. Hedy gasped at the sudden chill but simply snuggled more tightly against him. Carefully he drew the quilts back and arranged them around her.

She looked up at him. In the darkness she could not see his features. She could only feel him, his length beside her, his face above her own. Her hands were on the smoothness of his muscled shoulders. He gently gripped her upper arms.

"Hedy," he said, his voice low, "if we don't stop now, we're not going to stop. You know that, don't you?" He was leaning on his elbow, staring down at her.

"I know," she whispered.

He shook his head as if he were deeply troubled. His right hand moved up to caress, then rest against her jawline. She could feel the hair on his chest, tickling her bare skin ever so slightly. "Do you know how much I want you?" he asked, his voice full of longing.

She shook her head mutely, wishing she could see his face. She knew that he wanted her physically—but not if he wanted or desired anything more of her. She didn't know if he loved her, even a little bit, or if he ever could.

He traced the silken line of her eyebrow. "I wanted you from the moment I walked into this house and saw you standing there, your eyes full of blue storm clouds."

His hand moved across her forehead, stroking her bangs back, then he drew a finger along her other eyebrow. "I wanted you so much it scared me. I wanted you so much I kept trying to keep distance between us. It didn't work."

"I know," she breathed. She turned her face away, staring into the darkness. She had felt the same, so drawn to him it frightened her. The closer she allowed him, the more dangerous he was. Paradoxically she wanted him near.

"And yet," he murmured, lacing his fingers into her long hair, "whenever we start to get close, that doesn't work either. Something always veers out of control, goes wrong. Although I don't know what could be wrong with this—" he moved his body more snugly against hers "—or this..." he murmured, bringing his lips next to hers.

When he kissed her, Hedy shuddered almost convulsively. She didn't know whether she was shaken with desire, or fear, or a powerful combination of both.

He drew back again. "When I'm around you, right and wrong get tangled up. I don't know if we're too different or too much alike. I don't know if I should walk away from you and never look back, or if I should grab you and never let you go. Once I thought it'd be enough to sleep with you and get you out of my system. Now I'm not so sure. I don't even know how I feel about you. I don't know *you*, Hedy."

She was riven by confusion. Was he trying to warn her that if he made love to her it didn't mean "love," it didn't even mean "like," it didn't mean anything at all?

"If you don't know me, what are you doing in my bed?" she said tightly. "It's no longer considered chic to sleep with strangers."

He drew back farther, and she sensed anger in his movement. "There you go," he said between his teeth. "For a little country girl from Fox Creek, you're not exactly without defenses."

"I heard I needed defenses around you," she replied honestly. "I was told never to let them down."

He swore softly. He pulled away from her and fell backward onto the pillow as if defeated. "Jolene," he muttered with a groan. "I should have known."

But he kept one hand near her shoulder. She could feel its warmth. She rose on her elbow and stared down at him. His features were shadowy in the darkness. Sleet rattled against the windows.

"Jolene said you were in love with her. She said you never got over it. When she left her husband, all she had to do was call and you were there. It's true, isn't it?"

He was silent a long moment. "I loved her, yes. No, I never got over her. When she and Melvin separated I went to her because—look, it's complicated. I had to go. I don't know how to explain it." Ty, the master of words, found himself without any.

Hedy's heart turned leaden. "She said—"

"I don't want to talk about Jolene," he growled. Before she could protest or elude him, he put his arm around her neck and drew her down so that her face was only an inch from his. "She doesn't matter. I want to talk about us. Are you as confused about me as I am about you?"

"Yes," she whispered. She resisted the desire to reach out her hand and touch his lips. She wanted him to kiss her again, yet her body was tensed against his touch. She wanted to believe Jolene no longer meant anything to him, but she was afraid to.

He could feel the conflict that tautened her. Sighing harshly, he drew her down beside him so her head was nestled against his shoulder.

"Just stay here beside me, all right?" His arm held her close, a willing prisoner. The fingers of his other hand toyed with her hair again. "Just let you and me matter for now. Stay here with me, being warm. And together. That's all." His voice was weary.

Hedy made no reply. She laid her face against his chest once more. She listened to the strong and comforting rhythm of his heart. She could not deny herself the bittersweet pleasure of being held in his arms.

He had said he'd loved Jolene. He'd admitted he'd never gotten over it. He'd confessed he'd had to go to Jolene when she'd beckoned. And yet Hedy could not deny that something seemed to exist between Ty and herself, something powerful.

She realized, with shame, that he could have seduced her. She would have let him—she had been more than willing. But he had not. He was asking nothing more of her except closeness, human warmth. And she wanted to give them to him.

Right and wrong were mixed up inextricably in her heart. "I love you," she wanted to say. But she said nothing.

SHE AWOKE BEFORE HE DID. Startled and ashamed, she pulled the sheet more tightly around her. Under its cover, she buttoned her open shirt. But she could not yet move away. She watched him sleeping. She had never before noticed how long his lashes were. Brown stubble shadowed his jaw, making it look leaner than usual. His hair was tousled and fell over his forehead.

She wanted to reach out to stroke his hair back from his brow, or run her fingertips over the roughness of his unshaven jaw.

Instead she rose swiftly. She stepped into the shoes she didn't remember kicking off, then quietly gathered clean clothes. She looked around the shabby little bedroom. The walls were bare and the plaster patched. The air was so cold she was surprised she couldn't see her breath.

She was glad with all her heart that she and Ty hadn't made love. There had been something desperate, almost driven in the way they had ended up in bed. And yet she had loved lying all night in his arms. She let herself take one last glance at him stretched out in her bed. Then she slipped into the bathroom to shower and dress.

She donned clean jeans, a pale blue cotton turtleneck and a dark blue sweater. She brushed her hair and put on her lipstick. She studied her reflection in the mirror. The mirror showed her Hedy Hansen, a girl with golden-brown hair and blue eyes, but the eyes, as usual, looked worried.

The man she loved was sleeping in her house, in her bed. He had not made love to her, although she instinctively knew he would if she desired it. Did she desire it, desire him? Yes. No. Yes.

"What next?" she asked the girl in the mirror.

The image said nothing. It simply stared back with those troubled eyes.

She waited until she heard Ty moving about before she started breakfast. He slept late, until almost ten o'clock. He must have been exhausted, she thought, and he'd be starved as well. She turned on the oven and put in a batch of biscuits. She started grilling the bacon and mixing the eggs to scramble. She had no real coffee, so she opened her long-hoarded can of frozen orange juice to make up for the lack.

She was stirring the eggs into the frying pan when Ty appeared. He came up behind her and put his arms around her waist, then leaned down and pressed his prickly cheek against her smooth one and kissed her on the ear. She wanted to turn and put her arms around his neck. She stirred the eggs instead.

"Smells great," he whispered in her ear. "This is one of the advantages of finding a farm girl. She knows how to make a guy a real breakfast."

Tingles of desire danced along Hedy's spine and radiated throughout her body. "That's probably the most sexist remark in the history of Chicago," she murmured, not wanting him to know how powerfully his slightest touch affected her.

He laughed and kissed her ear again. "Sexist? I hiked ten miles in the snow for you. I held you all night long and didn't make love to you. If I got any more noble, women all over America would raise monuments to me. You're going to hold one crack about breakfast against me?"

"No." She smiled. He could always make her smile.

"Then stop staring into those eggs and kiss me."

He turned her to face him. He took the spatula from her hand and set it on the counter. "Good morning," he murmured, winding his arms around her. He bent and kissed her. Hedy felt as if she were being filled with bliss and light. Being in Ty's arms felt like coming home. She forgot about the eggs until they began to burn.

But once they were sitting across from each other at the breakfast table, Hedy felt awkward again.

"What's wrong?" he demanded, spreading jam on a biscuit. "You can't feel guilty. We didn't do anything."

Hedy cast him a guarded look. "We spent the night together," she said, then ducked her head and stared at her plate. "We slept together."

He shook his head. "You really are an innocent, aren't you? Don't tell me you want me to make an honest woman of you. I haven't made you dishonest—yet."

"What?" She blinked at him, not quite comprehending what he meant.

"I mean," he stated sardonically, "this doesn't mean we're engaged, you know. I have the classic bachelor's attitude toward marriage. I'd rather be thrown to ravening sharks."

Hedy set down her fork. "Who said anything about marriage?" she asked. Her cheeks burned and she knew she was blushing.

"I did," he replied easily. "I said it terrifies me. I mean, I should tell you that up front, right?"

She picked up her fork and feigned interest in her food. "Why should I care what you think about marriage?" she asked coolly.

He savored another bite of biscuit. "A woman should always care what a man thinks about marriage—if they're going to be involved."

"Oh?" She tried to keep her voice calm and light. "We're going to be involved?"

"Yes," he answered, his eyes meeting hers. "We are. I think we need each other."

His gaze remained locked with hers. Nervously she licked her lip. "Why do I need you?" she asked, her chin high.

"To teach you how to have fun again," he answered. "To enjoy life. Something's been too hard on you. Maybe one of these days you'll trust me enough to tell me what it is."

She shrugged, looking away. She wanted to tell him everything, yet she didn't trust herself to do so. She was afraid she would cry, and she didn't want that to happen. If she told him, she wanted to be in control of herself, using her head, not tortured by her heart.

"And why," she asked, trying to keep the tremble out of her voice, "do you need me?"

He studied her for a long moment. "I don't know," he said finally. "Maybe to remind me there's a serious side to life. I've made a profession of trying to forget it." Then the familiar cynical gleam returned to his eye. "Maybe I just want you for your biscuits. And your body heat. They're both delicious."

He left her after breakfast, promising to come back. He had animals to tend to, his car to see to, and his family to check on. Hedy watched out the window as he strode back to his own house. The day was gray, with a lowering sky that threatened more snow. She had noticed neither the grayness nor the cold when Ty was there. Whenever he was around, she felt as if she were standing in the sunshine.

But, she thought, troubled again, they had not spoken one word about Jolene this morning. And she still hadn't been able to reveal anything about her own past. Perhaps what had happened between them was only lust. She had to be careful.

Up the street, Mr. Hartford, who was retired, braved the cold and propped a ladder against the side of his house. He was getting ready to hang Christmas lights.

Hedy couldn't help it; the sight depressed her. This was her first Christmas without her mother, her first away from Fox Creek. Memories pricked at her like shards of glass.

She turned away from the window. The house was chilly.

Today she should start hanging the wallpaper in the bedroom, but she did not want to spend time in the bare little room. It would make her think of Ty, and she was afraid to.

The emptiness of the house closed around her. She would work on the kitchen cabinets today, a task she had been only too happy to put off.

Maybe hard work would keep her from thinking about what he had said about Jolene. At least, she tried to console herself, he was honest. The problem was that she kept forgetting about Jolene altogether. Now Jolene had gone back to her husband and Ty said he wanted a relationship with Hedy. And she couldn't deny she wanted one with him.

Ty didn't come back until shortly before dark. He kissed her hello, and once again Hedy experienced the shock of finding his lips at first winter-cold, then warm as sunshine.

He hugged her, looking around the kitchen askance. "What are you doing now?" he demanded. "Don't you ever stop slaving?"

"I can't," she answered. She loved the scratchy texture of his sweater against her cheek. "That's what I'm supposed to learn from you, remember? How to slow down and have fun again."

"I remember," he replied, holding her close. His voice had gone serious again. "Hedy—I wanted to be with you tonight. I can't. I can't see you for the next few days."

She looked up at him, hoping the disappointment didn't show in her face.

His own expression was somber. "We've had a family crisis. My Uncle Tymek died this afternoon. We were close when I was growing up. My Aunt Rosie'd like me there. My sister Lilka wants to fly down with me. The funeral's in Orlando. I'll be gone three days. I'm sorry to do this to you."

His face seemed to show real concern for her. "It won't be easy leaving you, but I have to go. My Aunt Rosie's been through a lot. My uncle was a good man, the best. If there's a heaven, he's there. I owe it to him to help out Rose back here on earth."

Hedy nodded, a lump in her throat. Ty's kindness, his sensitivity always took her by surprise. They seemed at odds with the mocking face he presented to the world, and the more touching because of it. Sometimes she wondered if he were really a womanizer at all, only a man wary of the power of his own emotions, unwilling to care as much as he could.

"I'll miss you," she murmured.

He smiled down at her. "It'll give you a chance to think. About us. To sort through the confusion, so we can talk when I get back. I'd take you with me, but I'd rather have you meet my family when circumstances are happier. Because that's what I want—to make you happy. For as long as we're together. Whether it's a short time or a long time. Understand?"

She nodded again. "Tell your Aunt Rosie I'm sorry," she said. "I'll take care of your animals if you want."

"That's great." He kissed her on the forehead. "I'll miss you, beautiful. Don't work too hard. And don't look so sad. I told you, I want you happy. Okay?"

"Okay," she promised, not sure she could fulfill the request.

He dug into his pocket and handed her his extra set of keys. "My sister's family's got a set of keys, too," he informed her. "They may stop by my place. You'll recognize them probably. Don't have them arrested as burglars."

She nodded, gazing up at him, eyes misty.

"I've got to go," he said reluctantly. "I'm taking a cab to O'Hare. The plane leaves at seven-thirty. God, Hedy, I hate to leave you."

"I could drive you," she offered, wanting more time with him, even if it was in the tangled traffic of the expressway. "I got the car started."

"No," he stated firmly. "It's still too slick. I don't want you to. I called the vet, by the way. The cat's doing fine. You can pick her up in a couple of days."

They looked at each other. He smiled at her but his smile was edged with unhappiness. She tried to smile back. Wordlessly he took her in his arms and held her for a long time. "I've got to go," he said at last. He kissed her goodbye. "And you know what I'd like to see when I get back?"

"What?" she asked. She kept her hands on his shoulders, as if she needed to touch him as much as she could before he left. She kept looking into his eyes, as if she needed to fill her memory to the brim with the sight of him.

"I'd like to see this house lit up the way W.A. used to do it. If I came home and saw that, I'd know you'd be starting to put some of your sadness behind you. At least a little. Is it too much to ask?"

She shrugged, too choked to be able to speak.

"Goodbye," he said softly. He went out the door and left her standing alone. As she watched him go, darkness was falling fast. It seemed to be falling into Hedy's heart as well.

She went to the front room and stared moodily out the window. The house was cold, as usual, and she crossed her arms, suppressing a shiver.

Up the street the Christmas lights at the Hartford home flashed on. The effect was dazzling. The house seemed made of tiny lights, all blue.

A life-size Santa Claus, complete with sled and reindeer, waved jovially from the center of the Hartford lawn. As a final touch, thousands of blue lights spelled out Tidings of Comfort and Joy across the roof.

Hedy stepped back, as if to distance herself mentally from the shining house. *Comfort and Joy,* she thought, biting her lip. This season had seldom brought her either.

But maybe Ty was right. She should learn to leave the sorrows of the past behind. She should join her neighbors in making this gift of light to others. But perhaps she would never be like other people—perhaps it was impossible.

It was growing late. With Ty gone, the house seemed to be so full of loneliness it smothered her. Hedy couldn't face stripping the kitchen cabinets, not until tomorrow. She had seen Marilyn Hong's lights on up the street. Marilyn had offered to lend her a sewing machine. Hedy was tired, but perhaps she could begin to make some curtains.

Her phone was still not working, so she walked to Marilyn's and asked if she could borrow the sewing machine. Marilyn's husband Sam, slightly rotund but extremely genial, insisted on carrying it back to Hedy's house for her.

He set it in the dining room, where the temperature was warmest. "You've done wonders," Sam said, his dark eyes roaming the walls. "I know how much effort this took. You're working a miracle."

"You really think so?" Hedy asked, pleased. "I know so," Sam told her. He rubbed his mittened hands together. "But it's chilly. You still have this old heater? Ty and I both tried to talk W.A. into replacing it. I don't trust it. I have a small electric heater I once used in my hobby room. I'll let you use it. That should help."

"You and Marilyn are both too kind," Hedy protested. "You'll spoil me." He only smiled.

The next day Marilyn came over, carrying the small heater. "Sam's putting up the lights," she said, "and he raved about how much work you've done. Will you let me see?"

Hedy gladly gave Marilyn the grand tour and was pleased when her friend complimented her on her progress. Marilyn agreed to have a cup of tea, but said she couldn't stay long; she had to help Sam with the decorations.

The two women sat at the old dining-room table, where the old heater's warmth was strongest. "Sam was right," Marilyn said with a little shiver. "You do need extra heat. This old thing—" she gave the heater a distrustful look "—is a menace."

"I'm used to it," Hedy shrugged. "W.A. Tidwell put up with it all those years. I can stand it for a little longer."

Marilyn shook her head. "You're impossible, Hedy. Are you and my nephew being impossible, too? Or will the two of you see each other again?"

Guilt and embarrassment rolled over Hedy. She had completely forgotten about Alex, who, under ordinary circumstances would be a difficult man to forget. "Alex is wonderful," she told Marilyn. "One of the nicest men I've ever met. But—"

"But the magic isn't there?" Marilyn concluded wryly.

"I think of him as a friend," Hedy plunged on, more embarrassed still. "He's wonderful, but—"

"But the magic isn't there," Marilyn repeated. "I should have known. And you and Ty are still at an impasse?"

Hedy tried to smile. She failed. "I'm not sure where Ty and I are," she said honestly. "I—well, things are complicated. He admits there's this other woman, and yet—" She couldn't finish the sentence. *And yet I love him. It's wrong but I can't get him out of my mind or my heart.* She could barely admit it to herself, let alone Marilyn.

Marilyn tactfully changed the subject. "The Hartfords have all their lights up already," she observed. "Most of us will put them up this weekend. I hope it won't be too painful for you. If there's anything I can do—"

Hedy gave her a grateful look. "I'm going to try not to let it bother me," she said. "In fact—" she stopped, wondering if she should tell Marilyn.

"In fact?" Marilyn prodded gently.

"Ty had to go away. There was a death in the family." Hedy plunged on in a rush, so that her voice wouldn't choke as it usually did. "He said he wished that when he came back that I'd have lights up, too. And I know if I did, it'd show I was—well, coming to terms with the past, instead of letting it dominate me."

Marilyn nodded. "You're right, Hedy. When something frightens you, you should confront it. It's best to face it until it no longer has power over you. But it must be your decision. Not simply something Ty wants to see."

Hedy nodded. "I know. I'm not sure I can do it."

"If you decide you want to," Marilyn offered, "call on Sam and me. We'll be glad to help. But only if you really want to."

"Thanks, Marilyn," Hedy said with an affectionate smile.

After Marilyn left, Hedy went back to work on her new dining-room curtains. She sewed until her eyes smarted and her back ached.

When at last she was ready for bed, she took the Hongs' small electric heater into the chilly bedroom and plugged it in. She climbed between the crisp, cold sheets and lay staring up through the darkness.

Again she thought of Ty. She loved him, and she hoped that he might love her in his way. His way might not be like a more conventional man's. He was capable of kindness and tenderness. But he could be passionate, as well, dazzling Hedy with the ardor of his desire. He promised no commitments, he said nothing of everlasting love or a lifetime relationship. But he could teach her to live again, and to laugh, and to care.

Was that enough? one frightened part of her mind asked. It had to be, replied another, hungry for life. He couldn't love Jolene, not really. If he loved someone else, he could not treat Hedy as he did, look at her the way he did, kiss her the way he did. Maybe he had somehow finally reconciled himself to never having Jolene. Maybe he, too, was ready to let go of a haunted past.

She smiled into the darkness. She would try to perform an act of faith for him. She would put up all the lights before he came back from Florida. She would try to let go of all her old sorrows and losses. And maybe he, in turn, could truly let go of his.

Marilyn and Sam Hong came the next day and helped her untangle what seemed like miles of Christmas lights. They spent the afternoon laughing and getting in one another's way and running inside to get warm. They drank innumerable cups of hot tea.

Hedy still wasn't sure she could decorate the sick old spruce tree in her front yard—Christmas trees, even temporary ones, would always be traumatic for her. But when Sam offered to do it, she let him.

W.A.'s lights were multicolored. In place, they edged the roof, the windows, the door, and spangled the bushes that lined the front of the house. The yard ornaments were an old, but impressive set of almost life-size white figures of the three kings.

Like most of the other houses, Hedy's had a sign for its roof. It took all three of them to set it up, and Hedy was grateful for the Hongs' help. But the message puzzled her. It didn't sound familiar or even particularly Christmassy. The rich, jewellike hues spelled out Hail the New.

"I don't understand," Hedy murmured to the Hongs when the sign was in place. "What's it mean?"

Marilyn said she had forgotten, if she'd ever known. Sam gave Hedy a satirical grin. "Don't you know your own culture?" he teased. "It's from a Christmas carol, 'Deck the Halls.' The third verse. 'Fast away the old year passes, Hail the new, ye lads and lasses.' With a bunch of fa-la-las in between."

Hedy gave him a pert look. "How do you know so much?"

"Brains," Sam said smugly, tapping his forehead. "My superior male intellect."

"You need to be humbled," Marilyn said with stern dignity. Then, abandoning dignity, she bent over, made a snowball, and flung it at her husband. Hedy followed suit. Sam fought back with spirit until Hedy and Marilyn mounted such an onslaught he had to take refuge behind the hydrangea bush and surrender.

That night when she turned on all the lights, Hedy couldn't help feeling a rush of exhilaration. The old house was stunning, transformed.

Perhaps Christmas wouldn't be so bad after all, she thought. She couldn't wait to see what Ty would say about the lights spangling her home. "Hail the New" seemed the perfect message.

Or maybe the perfect message was shining now from the Melrose house. It was simple, but eloquent. In brilliant white lights one word was spelled out: Love.

CHAPTER TEN

BY SUNDAY NIGHT, the neighborhood was brilliant with lights. Part of Hedy was still a bit frightened of so much display, but another part beheld it in childlike awe.

The Hartford house was decked in lights of heavenly blue, the Melrose house in white and gold. The Hongs had opted for the traditional red and green, but their house had the most unusual motif. On the right side of the roof blinked the words Peace on Earth. On the left side blinked the identical message, only in a Chinese pictograph.

The Golds' message to the world was in orange and yellow lights and said Shalom, which meant Peace. The Jennings, who had moved to Chicago ten years ago from Alabama, opted for a green Merry Christmas, Y'all. The Washington family had lights of every possible color and a nativity scene on the lawn. Sam estimated that there were almost a hundred thousand lights shining on Holly Street.

Only a few houses were still dark, Ty's among them. Decorating, Marilyn said, should be finished next week, and the men of the neighborhood would put up the sign at the street's entrance and decorate the streetlights. Already, cars from other neighborhoods and suburbs were beginning to cruise Holly Street as people came to take in the festival of lights.

Ty called. Hedy's phone was functioning again at last. His voice sounded wonderful to her.

But Ty said he couldn't talk long; the house was full of relatives, although he had managed to find a fairly quiet spot. He would be home late Monday night, he promised, although so late he wouldn't see her until Tuesday morning.

Hedy didn't tell him about the lights. She wanted them to be a surprise, a way to welcome him home. Whenever she turned on the switch that lit them all up, she felt she had done something slightly heroic. She squared her shoulders, thinking of the message her home sent through the night, "Hail the New."

Monday afternoon, she steeled herself enough to do a little Christmas shopping. She went to the Water Tower Mall, where each shop window seemed decked out for Christmas more elaborately than the last. Angels and Rudolphs and Santas and snowmen with top hats seemed to have taken over the mall. And among them jostled the Christmas shoppers, more people than Hedy thought existed.

She found Tippy's son a wonderful miniature tractor, perfect in every detail. Deciding to be extravagant, she bought Tip and Norm a big box of Christmas candy to share with the rest of the family, although she knew they wouldn't be expecting a gift from her.

She looked longingly at the clothes in the shop windows and wished she could indulge herself in a new coat. She was sick unto death of her old red and black jacket. Maybe next year, she thought.

She wanted to buy something for Marilyn, but nothing even in the fabulous riches of the Water Tower area seemed right. Hedy decided to go to the older State Street area.

There, too, the department stores dazzled. In the largest, over a thousand real Christmas trees glittered with what must have been half a million ornaments. Hedy was troubled by this display and fled from it. But she gathered her courage and kept on shopping.

She found what she wanted, at last, at the Art Institute. Even the famed bronze lions who guarded the museum's entrance were celebrating Christmas, their necks adorned with beribboned wreaths. The museum's gift shop was crowded with customers, but Hedy managed to find a beautiful blue Chinese silk scarf ornamented with flowers and butterflies.

She was unsure what to buy for Ty, but decided on a set of brass bookmarks. Their design was adapted from a nineteenth-century book on ornamentation, and she fell in love with them on sight.

She headed home exhausted, broke, and happy. She had spent more than she could afford, but again she had faced Christmas and triumphed. She had even felt bold enough to buy a box of Christmas cards. She would send greetings to Tip, the old neighbors back in Fox Creek, and the new ones in Chicago.

She stopped at the vet's to pick up Security, who looked as good as new. Her five kittens were fat, healthy, and mewing loudly. Ty was right. They might not be purebreds, but they were extremely pretty. It would be easy to find someone to love them.

When Hedy got home and made a bed in the laundry room for the new family, she decided that motherhood had agreed with Security. The cat, formerly so aloof, was affectionate, even demonstrative with her kittens. She purred, as if she was proud of herself and her offspring. For the first time she seemed to respond to Hedy's caresses, half closing her eyes and purring even louder.

The phone's jangle interrupted Hedy's contemplation of the cats. She was pleased to hear Ty's voice. Her pleasure evaporated when she heard his message. "Have you looked out the window?" he asked.

"No," she answered, glancing out. All afternoon the wind had been rising, the sky growing grayer and colder, but she had paid no attention. She had been too full of inner warmth.

The wind had started gusting so hard that the strings of lights on the houses stirred, and the Hartfords' model of Santa and his deer swayed as if it was actually going to take off and fly. In the growing darkness, snowflakes began to appear, rushing like swirling phantoms.

"Our flight's delayed," Ty said. "It's some sort of freak blizzard. The weather's crazy even down here. Torrents of rain."

Hedy's heart contracted. Suddenly all the lights in the world couldn't make Holly Street cheerful. She wanted Ty home.

"I'll get there as soon as I can," he said huskily. "Are you all right?"

"I'm fine," she lied. "I've got the kittens. They're beautiful. And Security's recovered."

"You're not working too hard?"

"No."

"And you're staying happy for me?"

"I'm doing fine," she said. She almost smiled. He'd be surprised at how well she was doing.

"I miss you," he said.

"I miss you, too." She wished he would say he loved her. But he did not. He only told her goodbye.

"Goodbye," she murmured. When he hung up, the sound of the dial tone returning was like a death knell, Hedy thought. The house was too silent without the sound of his voice.

She changed clothes, then settled down to write out the Christmas cards. With Ty's return delayed, it seemed a greater chore than when she had first contemplated it.

Be an adult, she told herself sternly. Other people have had troubles at Christmas, without letting it ruin the season, or taking it out on everyone else.

So she sat, addressing the cards and stamping them. She made her way determinedly through her address book until she came to the entry for Jolene: Mr. and Mrs. Melvin Porter. She remembered guiltily that she'd bought nothing for Jolene for Christmas. She'd told herself it was because she couldn't find anything fine enough.

But the disturbing truth was that she feared Jolene. Ty had loved her, he might still love her, he might always love her. She might be the woman to whom he would always, in his heart, belong.

Her train of thought was becoming so unpleasant she decided the only answer was to lose herself in a task even more dreary. She put down her pen and went back to stripping the worn finish from the kitchen cabinets. The job was not only hard, but evil-smelling. She had to use chemicals so strong she needed rubber gloves to handle them.

She worked until almost midnight, then fell into bed exhausted. She arose the next morning to find seven inches of fresh snow on the ground and more falling. She wrapped her Christmas packages to Tippy's family, then walked to the post office to mail the parcel and her cards. She didn't want to dig her driveway out from beneath the snowfall or to chance the slick streets. She looked up at the falling snow and wondered if Ty's flight would be held up again.

The wind was rising when she reached home. She welcomed the shelter of the house, even if it was always cold these days. One card, Jolene's still remained, lying unsigned on the table. Hedy put it back into the box and the box into a drawer so she wouldn't have to see it. She ached for Ty to be home. We have to talk about this, she kept telling herself, almost like a litany. We have to talk.

She put Marilyn's and Ty's presents in the hall closet and got back to work on the cabinets. It was a grueling job.

The phone didn't ring until the evening darkness had fallen and all the lights on Holly Street were blazing. Tonight few people were venturing out to see them. The snow was whirling more thickly than ever.

Hedy picked up the receiver anxiously.

"Baby, it's Ty. I'm still caught. I can't get to you. Unless I try walking again."

Hedy smiled but felt the familiar emptiness. "Don't do that."

"Flights are stacked up badly. I hear O'Hare's a nightmare. I'll get to you as soon as I can. But it may be another day."

"Maybe *I'll* walk to *you*," she said, suddenly bold.

"Maybe we can both walk and meet in Georgia. Or maybe you'd better just stay put and wait. When I see you I'm going to want you all to myself. In total privacy. For a long time."

She colored happily at his intimation, and felt the old frisson of worry about how he really felt about her. But they spoke of other things. She asked him how his aunt was doing. He said fine. He asked her how Benchley and Mrs. Parker were doing, and she said fine. She even remembered to put Mrs. Parker's knit hat on her when she took the dog outside. He asked how Security and the kittens were, and she said fine.

They were silent a moment. The long-distance line crackled between them. "It's hard to talk to you," he said at last. "I'm thinking so much of holding you. Of not needing words."

"I know," she murmured and imagined herself in his arms again, lying warm against him.

WEDNESDAY WAS A LONG DAY, made longer by Ty's not calling again until after the evening darkness closed around the neighborhood. "Tomorrow," he said grimly. He sounded as if he were talking through clenched teeth. "I can't get out of here until tomorrow. Lilka might make it tonight, and I'm letting her go ahead because of her kids. But I'll be there tomorrow. Maybe late, but I'll be there. I miss you, honey. I miss you a lot."

"I miss you, too," she said tightly. Again she wanted to say she loved him. But he did not speak of love, so neither did she.

Thursday morning he called and said with luck he'd get out of Orlando by noon. With even greater luck he might make it to Chicago by midnight. His brother-in-law and a few of his nephews might be over to put up his lights for him. Otherwise he was going to be the last one in the neighborhood this year. "Except for you," he added hastily, "and I'll understand if you don't have yours up. You promised to think about it, though. Did you?"

"I thought about it," she said evasively. She still wanted to surprise him. The lights themselves were a sort of mutual Christmas present. He had given her the courage to put them up. She had done so to please him.

The rest of the morning seemed to take forever to pass. She went back to the everlasting task of the kitchen cabinets. She was going to quit working on them early tonight, she told herself. She wanted to shower and wash her hair and be fresh for Ty when he finally got home.

Shortly after noon she saw two men and two boys arrive. One of the boys was Stanley, and she soon saw the four of them dragging boxes of lights into the yard, untangling long strings of them, getting out ladders.

She tried to concentrate on her work. She would not let herself look at the clock. When she finally allowed herself a glance, it was almost four. Ty's relatives were still working next door, taking turns disappearing inside to warm up.

One more hour to work on the cabinets, that's what she'd force herself to do. Then she would indulge in the luxury of a long, hot bath. She offered up a silent prayer that Ty would make it home.

The phone rang.

The voice was a man's and it sounded jubilant. Hedy didn't recognize it at first. "It's me, Norm," he said. It was Tippy's husband, in Fox Creek.

"Norm," she said, pleased. "I've been thinking of you and Tip all week. How long before the baby's due?"

"She's here," Norm chortled. "A little girl."

"She's here?" Hedy queried, her brows drawing together. "Isn't it a little soon?"

"Yep," Norm answered, "scared the heck out of me. But everything's great. Tip's fine and the baby's fine. She's a beautiful little thing. Looks just like Tip. Just exactly like her. Every bit as pretty as her mama."

"Norm, that's wonderful," Hedy said, her throat tightening with happiness.

"Yes—and Hedy, since this baby seemed determined to be born in the Christmas season, I'd like her middle name to be Noelle. But Tip says she won't do it unless you say it's okay. She doesn't want a name that would upset you."

Hedy swallowed hard. She was becoming more and more ashamed of her obsessive fear of Christmas. It shouldn't affect other people's lives. It shouldn't interfere with a proud father naming his child exactly as he wished.

"Oh, Norm," she almost whispered, "please do it. Tell Tippy I'll love that baby all the more for having Noelle in her name. Something good's finally happened at Christmas, and she's it."

"Good," Norm answered. "Then she's going to be Hedy Noelle. How do you like that?"

She smiled and swallowed hard again. "I love it."

"And we love you," Norm said, his voice thick with emotion. "Hedy, I'm not going to talk any more. I'm exhausted. I'm going home and crash smack into the mattress and stay there for twelve hours straight. How come nobody ever gives new fathers any sympathy?"

"I don't know," replied Hedy with a laugh. "Personally, my sympathy's with Tip. But have a good sleep. And love to all of you."

She hung up the phone. *Hedy Noelle,* she thought, smiling. A Christmas baby with her name—would wonders never cease? A new child, another new beginning. She smiled again. She was beginning to understand how Christmas was supposed to feel.

The sky was gray and night was falling fast. Hedy worked on her kitchen cupboards for another hour, then took a long, steaming soak in a bubble bath. She washed her hair and blew it dry so that it fell to her shoulders in silky brown-gold fullness.

Her closet offered only limited choices, so she put on her best jeans and her red sweater. She settled down on the couch with the novel she was supposed to read for English class.

Glancing out the window at the sky, now dark, she knew the hardest part of the evening was beginning: the waiting. She didn't know what she would say to Ty when she saw him again. Perhaps she would say nothing at all, just throw herself into his arms.

Security, taking a brief respite from motherhood, jumped onto the couch and nestled against Hedy, purring loudly. Touched, Hedy smiled again and stroked the cat. "Welcome home," she said softly. The cat snuggled more closely.

Dutifully, Hedy read two more chapters of the novel, although she found it hard to concentrate. When the phone rang again, she gave a little jump of alarm. What if Ty were still stranded in Orlando? What if he weren't on his way home after all?

Apprehensively she picked up the receiver. "Hello?"

"Hedy? Hedy Hansen?" asked a man's voice. It was deep, raspy, and curiously ill-tempered.

"Yes?"

"Hedy. I know about you." The man sounded gruffer still. "But you don't know me. I'm Melvin Porter. Jolene's husband."

Hedy was taken aback by surprise. Melvin was almost a mythical figure to her. She had never met him. "I'm glad to talk to you," she said, her pleasure genuine. "I hope you're well." She knew Melvin suffered bouts of ill health.

"I'm feeling better than anybody probably wants me to feel," Melvin growled. "I'm feeling just fine. I finally let them take out my gallbladder. Now I'll probably live forever."

Melvin sounded so irritable that Hedy was puzzled. She tried to offer a polite reply. "I hope—"

Melvin cut her off abruptly. "Let's talk straight. She's with him. I know it and you know it. Don't try to cover for them. It won't work."

"I—" Hedy stuttered in confusion, "I don't know what you mean."

"I mean Jolene and that damned columnist, that professional smart guy, that Marek. He's with her in Florida, isn't he? His phone number isn't listed, and his paper won't give it to me. But I found it in Jolene's book. He doesn't answer, he's not at home. He's with her, the damned fool.''

"I—I really don't understand.'' Ty and Jolene together in Florida? Hedy couldn't believe it. She refused to believe it.

"I said that wise guy Marek's run off to Florida after my wife. You've been her special little friend lately. Well, you get a message to them—to both of them.''

"I don't know what you're talking about,'' Hedy protested, shaken.

"I'm talking about this joker who's in love with *my* wife—and I mean mine—bought and paid for. I know he made a beeline for her the last time she walked out on me. They're together again, aren't they? I know she's in Florida. He went after her, didn't he?''

"No—yes,'' Hedy mumbled. "I mean, he's down there—''

"You knew he went after her, like a sneaking thief, the last time we fought, didn't you?'' Melvin demanded. "When she moved into the Mayfair?''

Hedy was breathing hard, as if she herself were guilty of something terrible. "Yes,'' she admitted softly. She had allowed herself to forget how shamelessly Ty had run to Jolene. She hadn't wanted to remember.

"For years this man has hovered over my marriage like a vulture. For years he's wanted her. That's why I made her sell that damned house. I didn't like him that near her. But what does she do? She turns around and sells it to you—her cousin, her cohort. You've been the go-between for the two of them, haven't you?''

Hedy put a hand on her stomach. She was feeling slightly sick. "No,'' she said, trying to defend herself. "I thought you and Jolene were reconciled.''

"So did I,'' Melvin snapped. "She'd promised not to see him again. I promised her she could keep her stupid real-estate business—even though it loses money hand over fist.

The only profit she's made all year long is on that house she sold you. She's no businesswoman. But she likes to pretend, and I let her pretend."

"What?" Hedy breathed, doubly shocked. She couldn't completely comprehend what Melvin was saying.

"I'm telling you that you shouldn't bother to cover for her," Melvin informed her, his voice almost malicious. "When she sold you that house, she took you for all you were worth. And then used you to keep Marek at her beck and call. Well, Miss Hansen, better you lose money on that dump than me. I've paid for enough of Jolene's 'renovations' and 'redecorating.' I told her she could keep the real-estate business. But this pouring money into old houses just for the fun of it has got to stop. Will she be realistic about it? No, she gets in a snit and runs off to Florida. Then I find out that he's gone, too. She confided in you last time—she told me. And she probably did this time. Where are they?"

Hedy put her hand to her forehead. Confusion and disillusionment whirled around in her brain, and a pain drilled between her eyebrows, so sharp it made her feel faint. "I don't know. I never knew they were together. He's in Orlando," she managed to utter. "He—he keeps saying he was delayed."

"Delayed," Melvin stormed. "I'll say he's delayed. And I know what delayed him. My wife. I can't even blame her. The bastard's been bombarding her with letters. Flattering her and undermining me. He'll do anything to get her away from me. Well, he can't. And he'd better understand it."

"Letters?" Hedy said numbly.

"Letters," he assured her. "They're sitting right in front of me—I found them in her jewelry drawer. It's like she wanted me to find them, dammit."

Hedy was silent. The pain between her eyes grew so intense it was blinding.

"Letters," Melvin fumed. "He writes her. Drivel is what he writes her. 'My Only One.' Pah! 'I want you to lie in my arms all night long, to feel your perfect body next to mine.' Sneaking twaddle! This man is no respecter of property—and Jolene is my property."

Hedy felt betrayed, humiliated. "I don't want to hear this. It's too—personal. You should talk this over with Jolene. With both of them."

"I can't *find* them," he nearly snarled. "I'm not afraid to confront him. Or her. Jolene and I have an agreement. She can have her fun as long as she's discreet. But she's not going to flaunt this man in my face. Because that's all it is—flaunting. She'll come back to me. She always does. Because of the money. She knows it and I know it, and Marek better damn well realize it, too. So you tell him—tell them both—that this can't go on."

"Please," Hedy said desperately. She pressed her hand harder against her forehead. "I've got nothing to do with this. If there's anything between them, then the three of you should—"

"You tell him to come and face me, man to man. You tell him—"

"I'm not telling anybody anything," Hedy protested. "This isn't my business. Please, Melvin, calm down—for your own sake."

"I'm fine," Melvin retorted. "Tell her to get herself home. And tell him to come see me, Melvin Porter. To come here like a man—if he dares. How could she love him? A coward like that? He doesn't understand her. I do. Tell him—tell him—she's mine, dammit. And the marriage license is my bill of sale."

The line went dead. He had hung up on her. For a moment Hedy kept clutching the phone, as if to assure herself that the call had really happened.

Feeling hollow and degraded, she put the receiver back in its cradle. So Ty was with Jolene again. Jolene had called, and he had gone, just as he had done before. Perhaps there wasn't even an Uncle Tymek, an Aunt Rosie. Ty was a man whose business was making words serve his purpose. What were lies, but words cleverly twisted?

She bowed her head. Darkness seemed to swirl about her. Was Jolene's success really just a fraud, something Melvin bought and paid for to keep her amused? Had Jolene really cheated her on the sale of the house?

That news alone would have made her feel sick with betrayal, but it was the thought of Ty that hurt most. Why had he bothered to lie? Why had he bothered to call her from Orlando?

There was only one answer. He wasn't certain Jolene was his. She had granted him another rendezvous, that was all. Until he knew he had her, he would keep his other women. If Jolene walked away from him again, Hedy would be there, silly and naive and adoring, almost begging to be used.

Lies, she thought. He had told her lie after lie after lie. The letters to Jolene were proof of that. But Hedy had believed him.

She moved to the window and stared out into the darkness. The neighborhood was filled with light, but it was meaningless light.

"Tidings of Comfort and Joy," said the Hartford house. "Love," said the Melrose house. But Hedy was sure she would never feel comfort or joy or love again. Her heart had turned to ice. This time it would remain ice. Forever.

CHAPTER ELEVEN

HOW STUPID, HOW TRUSTING and simple could she be? Hedy asked herself. How could she have ever expected any good to have come from Ty Marek? Hadn't Jolene herself warned her, time and again?

She rose and tried to turn up the heater, but it only sputtered harder.

I came to this city to restore this house, she thought grimly. And that's what I'm going to do. She would succeed because she was determined to do so. Her will had to be unwavering, unconquerable.

She returned once more to the job she hated most, the kitchen cabinets. But she worked mechanically, like a robot.

At almost midnight she heard a car pull up in front of her house. She heard the slamming of its door. Then there were footsteps on her porch, an impatient knocking at her door. She stood still for a moment, feeling the ice around her heart harden.

She took off her right-hand glove, and holding it, went to the door. She pulled it open. Ty stood there. She stared up at him, wondering how he had the nerve to show himself. Had Jolene rejected him again? Or was he simply amusing himself until she could divorce Melvin?

He didn't even notice her icy expression. He swept her into his arms, and she felt a wave of revulsion. She held herself as stiffly as a stone statue.

"If I hugged you as hard as I wanted to, I'd break you in two. Give me a kiss. One that lasts for a week."

He bent to kiss her, but Hedy drew back from his embrace. "What's the matter?" he asked, frowning slightly. "I'd kind of hoped to find you at my place. In a negligee, not rubber gloves. What's wrong? Why do you look that way?"

"You lied to me." The steadiness of her voice amazed her.

His frown deepened. "What do you mean, lied?" He kept his hands on her shoulders, as if to keep her from running away.

"You lied," she repeated sharply. "Jolene was in Orlando, wasn't she?"

His face went taut. "How did you know? Does Melvin know?"

Hedy laughed with contempt. "Does Melvin know?" she echoed scornfully. "Yes. He called here. So there's really no need to deny it."

He gripped her shoulders harder. His face looked almost haggard, but his expression was harsh, his jaw clenched. "Now listen, Hedy—"

"You *lied* to me," she repeated angrily, shaking her head to emphasize her disgust.

"I didn't lie," he argued, his mouth taking on a stubborn slant. "I just didn't say she was there. You don't understand—"

"I understand perfectly."

"Do you? That's funny, because Melvin apparently doesn't."

"Why are you back?" Hedy demanded calmly. "Did she change her mind again? Is she going back to him?"

"Yes," he answered curtly. "She is. If he'll have her."

"So she's through with you—until next time. You ought to be ashamed. She's married."

"Dammit, Hedy," he growled. "Will you listen? Just listen? It's finally over with Jolene—finally, after all these years."

"You'll never be free," she answered scornfully. "And you'd better stop sending her letters. Melvin found those, too."

"Letters?" For a moment his expression looked truly blank. "Look. All right. I saw her in Orlando. But—"

"I'm not interested in a detailed description," Hedy said belligerently. "Have your little soap opera without me. I'm busy. Will you go now?"

"Dammit!" Ty's fingers sank into her shoulders and he shook her so hard it hurt. "Will you listen?"

"Oh!" Hedy retorted angrily. "Now it's physical abuse. Go ahead. I can't stop you. You're too strong. But inside, you're weak. You're a cheat and a coward and a liar."

He stared down at her, his green-brown eyes narrowed. His mouth was cruel. "And maybe you're a possessive, suspicious little witch. Maybe it's none of your business if Jolene was in Orlando. Maybe I don't have to tell you everything. Who do you think you are, my wife?"

She glared up at him, her jaw set as stubbornly as his. "I wouldn't marry you—" she muttered between her teeth.

He released his grip, stepping backward as if the touch of her repulsed him. "Yeah, yeah," he snarled. "I know—if I were the last man on earth. Original, Hedy, original. Would you listen for one minute?"

"No!" she replied. "Why? To hear more lies? You never stop. You probably lied about your uncle. You probably lied about going down there with your sister. You can't stop lying. Not even about small things."

Disbelief mingled with the fury in his face. "What?" he demanded. "Have you lost your mind? I've been trying for days to get back to you. You've breathed too many paint fumes, baby."

"I'm not your baby," Hedy said furiously. "If I was going to be anybody's 'baby,' it wouldn't be yours. You're not honest enough. You're not responsible enough. In short, you're not man enough."

She slammed the door. He kicked it so hard she thought it would surely splinter. She resisted the desire to kick it back.

She heard him stalk away. She wanted to cry, she wanted to scream, she wanted to giggle hysterically, because it really was quite humorous, how foolish she'd been to trust him. Except she couldn't laugh, because that would be releasing emotion, and if she began to do that, she was afraid she would also start to cry, and she realized that no matter what, she was safest if she felt only anger.

Trying to suppress the turmoil within, Hedy peeled off her other glove. She flung both of them into the dining room. They bounced off the old heater, then lay beside it, like a pair of stained and empty hands.

She went into the bathroom and opened the medicine cabinet. She was exhausted and she needed rest from her own emotions. There were still two pills in the bottle of sleeping tablets the doctor had given her to help her get through the week of her mother's funeral. She spilled them into her hand and swallowed them without water.

She didn't bother to change her clothes. She went to the bedroom and threw herself on the cold bed. She lay, staring at the darkness, waiting for sleep to rescue her. At last it came, irresistible and immeasurably deep.

THE WIND HOWLED around the house, but Hedy didn't hear it. The cold in the bedroom intensified, but she didn't feel it. Nor could she see the old heater in the dining room when it shuddered, then threw sparks out onto the chemical-soaked gloves lying near it.

First one glove, then the other, burst into flame. Hedy slept on. The worn carpet beneath the flaming gloves smoldered, caught fire. Smoke began to fill the house. Hedy did not stir.

Later, all she would remember was being lost in a universe overwhelmed by confusion. Sounds of destruction penetrated her consciousness: wood splitting, glass shattering. There was no air, only smoke. She was choking.

Then the smoke was gone, but she still couldn't breathe. Everything was cold, far too cold. It was cold and dark and frozen. A pair of arms held her prisoner and she had no strength to escape. She was trapped in a freezing, breathless nightmare.

She couldn't stop coughing and she couldn't get her breath. Then she was lying in the snow, in the incredible coldness of the snow. How silly and uncomfortable, she thought, to be lying in the snow.

She tried to raise herself. Orange lights danced before her aching eyes. Flames. They capered wildly in the darkness, flashing on the snow.

That was the last thing she remembered: that the snow itself seemed to be on fire. But it wasn't the snow. It was her house.

"YOU KEEP SAYING YOU WON'T see anybody," the doctor told Hedy. "It isn't good for you. You have to face what happened. You have to face people."

Hedy, sitting up in bed, her hair spilling down on the white shoulders of her gown, only shrugged. "I can face what happened. I know what happened. I just don't want to see anybody. Don't ask me to. I just want to go back to Fox Creek. That's all."

The doctor, Jon Forester, was young, plump, and sympathetic. He sighed. "The man who keeps trying to see you—"

Ty. Hedy wanted nothing to do with him. He had hurt her too deeply.

"I don't want to see him," she said shortly.

"He saved your life. He was the one who saw the fire. He kicked down the door and carried you out."

"Commendable," Hedy said bitterly. "Maybe somebody will give him a medal." She couldn't think about Ty. She couldn't think about anything. She would go back to Fox Creek and pretend none of this had happened.

"Hedy," the doctor wheedled, "he's come here every day for almost a week. Aren't you even going to thank him?"

"I'll write him a note." There was no Ty Marek, Hedy thought with stubborn intensity. She would pretend he didn't exist, had never existed.

"What about your friend?" the doctor asked, trying a different tack. "Mrs. Hong? She's been here every day, too. She's here now. She wants very much to see you."

Hedy swallowed hard. "I don't think I can. I think it's best that I just go home."

The doctor reached out a hand and touched Hedy's cheek, which had a slight cut on it. The cut, from when Ty had carried her out through a broken window, was the only visible sign of what had happened to her.

"Physically, you're almost well," he murmured. "Smoke inhalation, then a bad case of pneumonia, brought on as much by overwork as exposure. You've pushed yourself too hard. But you're young and you're strong and almost well. It's your attitude that worries me, Hedy. It's as if you've shut off all your emotions."

Hedy shrugged again. She stared down at the sheets covering her legs. "What good would it do to be emotional?"

Jon Forester shook his head. He put his hands into his pockets. "Hedy, Hedy," he sighed. "Nobody wants you to get emotional or hysterical. But you can't deny your emotions, either. You've been through a great deal—"

Hedy refused to look at him. He had large brown eyes, like a cocker spaniel. They were eyes that brimmed with feeling and Hedy wanted to feel nothing. "What I've been through is over," she said, sounding perfectly calm. "I'll go home. Where I belong."

She had talked to Norm in Fox Creek. He was concerned, unsure about her decision to leave Chicago, but he said he would come for her, and she was welcome to stay with him and Tippy as long as she wanted.

"What you've been through *isn't* over," Dr. Forester said firmly. "You've had a series of ordeals and losses. You keep trying to ignore them, but you've got to come to terms with them."

"I've come to terms," Hedy said with the same artificial calm. "Some things are best forgotten. I just want to go home."

"But is Fox Creek home, Hedy?" the doctor demanded. "What kind of life will you have there?"

She shrugged again, then squared her shoulders. "I suppose I'll be a sort of maiden-aunt type. I'll live with my cousin's family. I can pay my own way. And I know how to work a tree farm. It's what I know best. I should never have left."

The young doctor set his mouth grimly and shook his head again. "You're too young and attractive to talk about being a maiden aunt and hiding yourself away from the world."

"I'm *not* hiding," Hedy said, showing her first spark of emotion. She bit her lip. She made her face go blank again. "I'm being sensible, that's all. I'm using my head."

"When's he coming for you, this cousin?"

"My cousin's husband. Tomorrow. As soon as I'm released." She knew it was asking a great deal for Norm to come to get her and take her back to Fox Creek. But she would pay him back when she sold her property.

"And you're determined to sell that house?" John Forester persisted. "You won't go back, try again?"

She swallowed hard. "No. The woman from the insurance company said there are thousands of dollars' worth of damage. She said I'd paid too much for the house in the first place. It's hardly worth fixing. The furniture wasn't covered at all. I can't afford to start over. And I can't go through it again. I'll sell it as is. Someone can tear it down and build a new house. It's what should have been done in the first place."

"Hedy," Jon Forester said, "frankly, you worry me. You talk about all this as coolly as if you were a tape recording. You reject every attempt to reach out to you—"

Hedy looked around her room. It was cold and antiseptic. The only spot of brightness she had allowed was a pot of golden mums that Tippy and Norm had sent. She hadn't meant to be rude, but when flowers and cards came from other people, she asked the nurses to take them away. There had been flowers from the Hongs, even a bouquet from Alex, Marilyn's nephew. Peg Melrose had sent a plant, Emma Gold an arrangement of white chrysanthemums.

And Ty—oh, heaven, Hedy thought hopelessly, Ty had practically tried to fill the room with flowers and balloons and chocolates and teddy bears.

Hedy was touched in spite of herself, and because she was touched, she knew she must send it all away. There was a little girl on her floor with a broken leg. Hedy had all of Ty's gifts sent to the child.

Jolene had sent a single flower in a bud vase. She had also sent a note that she and Melvin had had another "little tiff," but were reconciled and vacationing in the Bahamas. Poor Ty, Hedy thought. He was shut out again. Until the next "little tiff." Then he would run to Jolene's side again. In the meantime he would attempt to play the considerate hero to her. It wouldn't work. He'd better go back to the park and set his snare for the Canarsi twins.

"Did you hear me, Hedy?" the doctor persisted. "I said you're rejecting all the attempts people make to reach out to you. You won't reach back. That's not healthy."

"I don't want to reach out to them," Hedy said. She discovered, to her humiliation, that she was suppressing a sob. "I can't reach out to them. It hurts too much. Can't you understand that? Can't you leave me alone? I don't want to think about it. I can't think about it. I have to go away and never look back—ever—can't you understand that?"

She tried to hold back another sob and was less successful. She bit her lip again, harder, this time. In spite of her efforts, tears rose to her eyes.

"Yes, Hedy," he said. "I'll leave you alone. But if you want to cry, you should cry."

He turned and left the room. He didn't know if she would cry or not. But he was incredibly relieved. For the first time in seven days, she had shown emotion. There was hope for her after all.

The round little doctor with the liquid brown eyes turned a corner and saw the woman sitting in the lounge area.

"How is she?" Marilyn Hong asked. "Will she see anyone yet?"

"No," he answered, patting her shoulder. "Not yet. But she's better. I really think she's better."

Marilyn's expression was concerned, almost harried. "Here," she said, reaching into her purse. "Give her these.

They're pictures of her cat and kittens. They're fine. One of the neighbors is keeping them for her."

"Thank you," Jon Forester said, glancing at the snapshots. "Maybe it will help. And I'm sorry she won't see you. It's just that I think at present she's trying so hard to stay in control that she's afraid to open herself to any emotional experience."

"I understand," Marilyn said.

"But I'm afraid she's still determined to go back to Fox Creek and retreat from everything that's happened. I think she's absolutely terrified of admitting she cares about anything."

Marilyn gave him a level look. "There's an old saying about what to do if someone draws a circle around himself that shuts you out."

The doctor raised an eyebrow. "Yes?"

"You draw a circle that takes him in," said Marilyn.

NORMAN PICKED HEDY UP the next day at eleven o'clock. She felt almost well and was embarrassed that the staff made her use a wheelchair to leave the building. "I only had pneumonia," she muttered. "People will think I was run over by a steamroller or something."

"In a way you were," Norm replied sardonically. He was a big, bluff young man with rosy cheeks and a black beard. "In terms of emotion, you were."

"I wish everybody would stop harping on my emotions," Hedy said, trying to sink lower in the wheelchair to reduce her visibility.

"Emotions are important," Norm stated calmly. "For instance, I like running a tree farm. You hated it. Do you really think you're going to be happy back in Fox Creek?"

"Happy," she replied between clenched teeth. "I'm not interested in being happy. I just want a nice, dull, boring sensible life."

"Hmm," Norm offered. "Funny. I'm happy, but I figure I'm lucky if life's nice and sensible about half the time."

He stopped the wheelchair at the edge of the parking lot, helped her out, and gave the chair back to an attendant. Hedy stood up. She felt a bit weak but otherwise fine, and it was good to be out of the colorless confines of the hospital.

Norm had brought her a new outfit to wear, even shoes and a coat and gloves. They were surprisingly stylish, all in a coordinated blue-gray that set off the more intense blue of her eyes. She wondered how Tip had ever found it in Fox Creek. Norm and Tip must have spent a fortune. She would pay them back as soon as she could.

Norm linked his arm through hers. He wore a plaid mackinaw and a knitted cap pulled down over his curly black hair. He walked her to a large silver Buick and opened the door on the passenger side.

She paused, looking at him in surprise. "This isn't your car," she said. "Is it?"

In confusion she noticed that another person was in the car, in the driver's seat. "It's all right, Hedy," Norm said gently. "Just get in."

Puzzled, she climbed into the car and sat down. She looked at the driver, a tall woman whose hair was hidden by a lovely black fox-fur hat. She wore a scarlet coat, expensively cut, with a black fox collar. Although the sky was gray, the snow still gleamed sharply, and the woman's eyes were hidden by large, stylish dark glasses. She looked vaguely familiar, but Hedy couldn't identify her.

"Hello, Hedy," she said. Norm climbed into the back seat directly behind Hedy.

Hedy looked back at him, feeling a slight rise of panic. "Norm, I thought you drove down to get me."

"I flew. Some people at this end arranged for this car. And the driver. Hedy, this is Lilka Vanacek."

"Hello a second time," said Lilka. She pushed her large sunglasses down on her nose. Hedy found herself staring into green-brown, slightly slanted eyes. *Lilka,* she thought, her panic real now.

"Right," Lilka said. "Ty's sister." She had the same irreverent crook to her mouth as Ty had, and the same amused lilt in her voice.

"I don't understand this," Hedy said at last. "How am I getting home? Norm, aren't you taking me home?"

"Sure, Hedy," he assured her. "It's just that you haven't been thinking clearly lately. If you want to go, we'll take your car. Otherwise, we'd have to tow it."

Hedy shook her head to clear it. Of course Norm was right—she hadn't been thinking clearly. She had forgotten completely about her car. She had just assumed it was ruined, along with everything else she owned. When Norm had called, volunteering to drive her back to Fox Creek, she hadn't given her own car a thought.

"Oh." She felt incredibly foolish. She stared down at the folds of her blue-gray coat. "I thought it was...I'm glad it's all right. But I still don't understand."

"Right," Lilka Vanacek answered briskly, putting the car in gear. "Why am I here? Why not Marilyn Hong? She wanted to pick you up, but I told her I wanted to talk to you. There are some things you need to hear. And I'm not shy about saying them."

Lilka wheeled out of the parking lot and manuevered onto the expressway with the Chicagoan boldness that Hedy had never mastered. Hedy folded her hands in her lap and looked numbly at the gray buildings that towered around them in the winter air.

Seeing Ty's sister threw her into turmoil. She wanted to flee, but she was trapped.

"Ty's worried about you. He cares about you a good deal," Lilka said frankly. "But, sweetie, it hasn't been easy on him. Because you scare him half to death."

"Me?" Hedy asked, giving Lilka a sidelong glance. "Scare him?" The idea seemed preposterous.

"Yes. You really do look the way Jolene used to, before she got so hard. Of all the women in the world, you'd set him most on edge, make him most defensive."

Hedy clenched her hands together even more tightly. She looked away from Lilka, stared unseeing out the window.

"Hedy," Lilka said firmly, "right now, you feel as if you've lost everything. As if you can't afford to care about anything—except maybe your immediate family. Well, Ty came out of that hospital eleven years ago. And he felt the same way. Exactly."

Hedy felt Norm's hand on her shoulder. "Be a soldier, Hedy," he said. "You need to hear this."

Lilka was expertly weaving the big car in and out of the traffic. "We're all doing all right now, we Marek kids," she said. "But we grew up without much money, without much of anything. The only way Ty could get to a good college was on a track scholarship. He was just a heck of a runner. It's a grueling sport, running. I've seen men finish a race and fall over into the cinders, crying from exhaustion. Ty wanted to keep that scholarship. He drove himself mercilessly. And I mean mercilessly."

Lilka adjusted her sunglasses. "And then," she continued, her tone resigned, "then he met her. Jolene. They were both eighteen. He fell hard. Well, Jolene got to him. And she changed him. To please her, he drove himself even harder. He started working nights, so he'd have money to take her out. He switched his major to pre-law, because Jolene didn't want a poor journalist, she wanted a rich lawyer. He was getting straight A's. He was working himself like two men."

Hedy stole another glance at Lilka. She looked calm, but the resentment in her voice was real. "I told him he was crazy. I told him she wasn't worth it. She was spoiled and grasping. But he got it into his head that he wanted her and he half killed himself trying to be what she wanted, to be able to give her the future she wanted."

"I still don't understand," Hedy murmured. The man Lilka was describing didn't sound at all like the Ty she knew.

"You ought to be able to understand as well as anybody," Lilka stated, then sighed. "Ty was working nights as a janitor at the college. It's the same job Papa did. Ty never stopped working. He could always fix anything, Ty could. But one night there was a freak accident. He and another student were cleaning the stage in the theater department. The other guy started fooling around with the ropes that held the sandbags, the weights that hang above the stage. He did something wrong and one fell. It caught Ty right in the back of the head. It broke his neck."

"What?" Hedy said, horrified.

"It broke his neck," Lilka repeated grimly. "We didn't know for a while if he'd ever walk again. We didn't know how well he'd be able to use his hands. But we all knew that even if he recovered, running was out. His scholarship was gone. He wasn't going to finish college after all."

Norm's hand tightened on Hedy's shoulder again. "She told me this story on the way to the hospital, Hedy. You'll understand a lot of things better when you've heard it."

"And where was Jolene when Ty was lying there wondering if he'd ever walk again?" Lilka asked bitterly. "Well,

Jolene just seemed to vanish. A bright young man with lots of money in his future was one thing. A guy flat on his back who'd just lost all his prospects was another. She came to see him exactly once. And she didn't waste any time. By the time Ty was out of the hospital, she'd married Larry Casper. He was already rich. He could give her all the things she wanted. Because Jolene didn't want love or loyalty. Jolene wanted things. *Things,*" Lilka repeated with contempt.

Hedy suddenly began to understand things that puzzled her before. Ty's pose of laziness. His pretense of never working or exerting himself. His refusal to take things seriously.

Lilka threw her a measuring look. "Your doctor's worried about you, you know," she said bluntly. "Your attitude. Your state of mind. You're retreating from feeling anything."

"Sometimes," Hedy almost whispered, "there's too much to feel. It—it scares you."

Lilka nodded. "I've seen it before, sweetie. I saw it with Ty. He did the same thing. Before he got so intense about college—and Jolene—he'd been a funny guy. He came out of that hospital hiding his feelings behind a laugh. And he's been hiding them ever since. Till you came along."

"Me?" Hedy asked dubiously. "But he never got over Jolene. He admitted as much himself."

Lilka kept her gaze on the traffic. She smiled without mirth. "He never got over her. In the sense that some people don't get over being in a war or a hurricane or an earthquake. It leaves its mark. She affected him, certainly. She made him wary of committing himself to any woman, of even pretending to be serious about anything. But he didn't love her anymore. How could he? After what she did?"

Hedy was starting to tremble. She didn't even understand why. She reached up and caught Norm's hand, hanging on for emotional support. "But when she and Melvin separated the first time, he went right to her. He stayed for—a long time with her," Hedy said.

Lilka shook her head. "Jolene's conceited, Hedy. She can't imagine any man falling out of love with her. When Ty started making it as a writer, he suddenly seemed interesting to her again. She bought that house next door to him thinking that he'd be panting at her heels in no time at all. She even convinced Melvin that Ty still wanted her. That's why he made her sell the house. When she and Melvin had that first flare-up, she called Ty and demanded he talk to her. He went. He told her in no uncertain terms that it was over, it'd been over for years. He didn't love her. He probably hadn't ever loved her—it was just infatuation."

"But—but he stayed with her," Hedy protested, confused.

"Wrong," she said emphatically. "He stayed in our cabin up in Kewaunee, Wisconsin—she couldn't even reach him by phone there. He went out of his way to stay out of *her* way. He wanted nothing to do with her games."

"I still don't understand," Hedy muttered. "Melvin called me. He was sure Jolene was in Florida with Ty. He said he'd found letters—"

Lilka's mouth twisted in disgust. "She heard Uncle Tymek died. She knew Ty would be down there. She and Melvin had a quarrel and she followed Ty to Orlando. Hedy, I was *there*. She kept calling Aunt Rosie's house, begging to talk to Ty. She just wouldn't believe she still didn't have him snared. Finally he agreed to meet her, but I went with him. I sat there, sweetie. I heard it all. He told her to go back to Melvin. He told her he didn't want her. He told her he'd found somebody else. Good lord, you should have seen her sulk."

"But," Hedy said hesitantly, "the letters that Melvin found. What about them? Did Ty write them?"

"Sure, Ty wrote her letters. Twelve years ago. Jolene probably planted them so Melvin would have a jealous explosion. You see, I think Melvin almost likes being jealous. He wants to believe his Jolene is so desirable that everybody else wants her. It makes him feel like an important man, and he's impossible to talk to when he's on one of his rampages. I have friends who know both of them well, Hedy. They're not America's happiest couple. But they may be its most self-centered."

Lilka sighed. Her expression softened slightly. "Ty finally went to Melvin this time. He confronted him. He told him clearly he wanted nothing to do with Jolene and for Melvin to leave you alone. He was forceful about it. Extremely. He made Melvin so furious that he packed up and dragged Jolene off to the Bahamas. And I heard he took her back with the condition that she give up all her little business hobbies and devote her life to paying attention to Melvin and Melvin exclusively, and Melvin twenty-four hours a day."

Hedy sat back against the seat, slightly stunned. She felt flooded with shame. "I wasn't fair to your brother," she said huskily. "I wasn't fair at all."

Lilka gave her a sympathetic glance. "You couldn't help it, sweetie. You and Ty are two of a kind. Bad things have happened to you both. You both try to deny emotions. Ty does it with laughter and jokes. You did it with work. But can't you understand now that although he was attracted to you, he didn't want to be. Good grief, you look like her, you're even related to her, and he kept thinking that you had to be like her in other ways. It's no wonder the two of you have had such an up-and-down relationship."

Up-and-down hardly began to describe it, Hedy thought sadly. And she noted with wariness that the car was nearing her street, her house.

She stiffened in fear. "No," she said in a small strangled voice, "I can't go back there. I can't see it again. You don't understand. I'm not strong enough for this. I have to just go home."

"And what," Norm asked softly, "if home is really Holly Street? The doctor thinks you ought to confront it, Hedy. We've talked to him about it. Besides, you may have more strength than you think. It's just not *where* you think."

Hedy looked wildly out the car's window. It was all too familiar. The memories crowded back with painful clarity. Again she was seized by the desire to flee. "I can't go back," she repeated desperately. "Lilka, stop, please—don't do this to me—please!"

CHAPTER TWELVE

"HEDY," LILKA SAID as gently as she could, "We're not doing it to you. We're doing it for you. I know what you're going through, believe me. I told you, I saw Ty go through it, too. For all his jokes, for all his pretending not to care, it took him two years to be able to walk past that college again."

Hedy sank lower in her seat. What Lilka said was true. What Ty had survived was worse than what had happened to her. She wondered if he would forgive her for the way she had acted. It was too much to hope for, so she did not allow herself to hope.

Lilka continued, "Norm said you were looking for strength in the wrong place. That's because you're looking only to yourself. It's time to look to others. They're stretching out their hands to you. It's not from pity, not from charity, it's from generosity and humanity. It's the greatest of gifts. It shouldn't be refused lightly."

"I'm selling the house," Hedy said, her voice shaking. "I have no choice. I can't do it again, start over from nothing—"

"Maybe there's more than nothing to start from," Lilka answered. "And maybe you underestimate yourself. Ty told me how much you accomplished. You did it once. You can do it again."

No, Hedy thought, *I can't.* And she knew she couldn't face the ruined house. It had cost her too much, physically, emotionally, spiritually. And she didn't dare think of Ty.

But the big silver Buick took the last turn and entered Holly Street. *Trapped,* Hedy thought, a choking sensation in her throat.

For the first time she saw the new sign at the entrance to the street. It was thickly bordered with holly that looked both rich and real. Its words sparkled in the noon light. At night its lights would shine out its message like a beacon: Holly Street Wishes Light and Life to All. Merry Christmas.

Hedy tried to swallow the lump in her throat and her vision blurred. Up the street, the lights of the Melrose house blinked on, even though it was still daylight. Love, they spelled out against the cloudy sky.

A second later the Hongs' lights twinkled on. Peace, they said. Almost immediately, the lights of the Hartford house sprang to life, announcing Tidings of Comfort and Joy.

Hedy turned away. She could not look. But she stole a glimpse at Ty's house. His message was so typically Ty it made the lump in her throat even worse. Huge red letters across his roof simply spelled out Ho, Ho, Ho.

All over his snowy lawn were large, strange, fantastical flowers, a whimsical garden of huge artificial blooms, rich with red and gold petals and glossy, green foliage. Giant, spangled gold and black bees seemed to hover among them, their antennae bobbling foolishly. Models of impudent-faced elves tended this wealth of amazing flowers.

Once, Hedy would have been amused and delighted by such a marvelous sight. But something in the scene disturbed her; something was not normal. It was Ty's house, she realized numbly. It was no longer orange. It was an ordinary, respectable white.

Uneasily she allowed her attention to rest at last on her own house. There were black marks on the clapboards near the west windows, reminders of the smoke that had poured out that terrible night. But the structure didn't seem nearly as damaged as she imagined.

Suddenly her own house's lights flickered on and blazed out their message, Hail the New. The three kings, a bit worse for wear, still marched stoically across the snow.

"My house," Hedy said nervously. "The lights went on. Somebody's inside."

"Could be," Lilka answered calmly, stopping the car in her driveway. "Let's see."

Hedy grabbed at her sleeve. "I can't," she said, panic flooding her again. "I can't. Really."

Lilka looked at her, sympathy in her green-brown eyes. "You can. You have to, Hedy. You'll understand. Come."

She got out and so did Norm. He opened Hedy's door. He took her hand and helped her out. He linked his arm through hers, and walked her to the front porch. Her legs were shaking so badly that halfway there he had to put his arm around her. The porch was scuffed and smoke was ground into its aging paint. The front door was new and still unpainted. Norm pushed it open.

"Merry Christmas, Hedy," Norm said gently as he steered her into her front room. "From your neighbors."

She blinked in surprise. The room was almost as it had been before the fire. The woodwork was once again pristine and perfect. New wallpaper, exactly like that she had hung, covered the walls. Only the old carpet was gone, but the wooden floors beneath had been repaired, sanded, and were waiting for varnish.

She felt light-headed, as if she were going to faint. It was like stepping into the past, before the nightmare of the fire. It could not be real.

The dining room, too, sparkled with fresh paint, paper, and trim. The ancient heater was gone. The walls and floors here were not completely repaired, but progress had been made. Her dilapidated furniture had disappeared, but different furniture, some of it familiar, replaced it.

Hedy passed her hand over her eyes. Perhaps she was still in the hospital and this was some sort of fever dream.

Lilka opened the door to the kitchen. The sad old linoleum had been torn up, replaced by black and white tile. The burnt cabinets were gone, and new ones of shiny black enamel hung in their place. The old stove and refrigerator had been scrubbed until they sparkled, and the dingy wallpaper had been replaced with a snappy pattern in white, black and red.

"Lilka," Hedy said, "who did this? And how?"

"Holly Street did it," Lilka said. "Mr. Hartford owns a cleaning company. He brought in a crew to get rid of the worst of the mess. Bob Melrose owns a decorating company. He donated the material and labor for the walls and the floors. The Hongs, the Golds, and the Melroses spent an entire weekend working on the rest of it. And my husband helped. He's a building contractor. The furniture, well, there's a little from everybody. That's the Washingtons' easy chair. The Browns' dining-room table. Marilyn Hong tried to get your curtains done, but she didn't finish. She and Mrs. Hernandez are still working on them."

Hedy looked in dazed disbelief. The house looked better than it had before the fire. Norm gave her an awkward squeeze.

"Not everything got done, but most of it did," Lilka said. "It was done without consulting you. But you wouldn't talk to anyone. I hope you don't hate it."

"I love it," Hedy breathed, then humiliated herself by bursting into tears. She had turned her back on everyone on

Holly Street, but they had refused to turn their backs on her. They had come to share their time, their work, their talent, their goods, their money. And their love.

"Don't cry," Norm said uncomfortably. "What's wrong? You're sad? I thought you'd be happy. Oh, gosh, Hedy, you know I can't stand to see a woman cry. Here's a handkerchief—take it, take it—please!"

Gratefully, Hedy took the handkerchief, then started to cry even harder. The dam that she had erected to restrain her emotions had broken at last.

"Don't cry, don't cry, don't cry," Norm begged. He was so distraught he was almost in tears himself. "We had to show you—the doctor said you wouldn't listen to anything, but seeing might shock some sense back into you. Like a fool, I believed him. Now what have we done?"

"A fine job, Norm," said a familiar voice. "But I think I'd better take over now. You're right. You can't handle a crying woman. This is how it's done."

Ty Marek stood in the door of the hallway. He had a smudge of dirt on one cheek, a hammer thrust into his belt, and his hair hung in his eyes. He walked slowly to Hedy and took the handkerchief from her. He put his arm around her and gently wiped her eyes. "It's okay," he said softly. "You're home now."

Hedy was still too stunned to resist. She gave herself to his embrace as if she were surrendering to fate itself. "What are you doing here?" she asked, her voice muffled against his chest. "Oh, Ty. Oh, Ty."

"Trying to vent your new furnace," he said, patting her back. "Know what? It isn't any fun."

"Furnace?" she asked. She looked up at him. Was she really in his arms, she wondered dizzily. Was it really that easy?

"The furnace is Ty's contribution," Lilka explained. "He's completely ruined his image. He's worked days on the thing. Banging and clanging and fussing and cussing."

"Ty," Hedy said softly, shaking her head in wonder, "why are you slaving like that? You *hate* this sort of thing."

"I hate this sort of thing, all right," he said, taking Hedy's face between his hands. "But I love you. That's why."

She stared up at him dumbfounded. Her eyes misted over again.

He licked his lips. He swallowed. "I figured I'd better say that in front of witnesses," he muttered. "Just so there's no more confusion. Maybe I'd better say it again. I love you. Only you."

"And I," Lilka said, suddenly brusque and businesslike, "have to go. Norm and I are supposed to have tea at Marilyn Hong's. We'll be there if you want us for anything. You two need to be alone. Goodbye for now."

"Goodbye," Hedy murmured. Ty simply gave them a crooked smile. "Alone at last," he whispered as Norm softly shut the door, casting them one last, shy glance.

"I'm sorry, Hedy," Ty said, his smile fading. "About the night of the fire. I should have been more patient. I should have made you listen. But I was tired and I didn't know what was going on. And to tell the truth, I was still wary about caring about you as much as I did. I guess I didn't know how much I loved you until I looked out and saw the smoke coming out of the house. The thought of losing you—"

He wrapped his arms around her more tightly. "The thought of losing you was worse than any physical pain I've ever known." He laid his cheek against her hair. She could feel the strong beat of his heart against her own. "And then, when you were in the hospital, I thought, what if I lose her now? I thought, what if she slips away from me, from all of us? I couldn't stand that, either."

Hedy kept her face pressed against his chest. "I was afraid to care, too. I was terrified. I guess I started thinking that every time I loved something, I lost it."

He groaned slightly and pulled her closer still. "I know. I understand. I've been there. And it's a lousy place to be, Hedy. Let's not either of us ever go there again."

She could say nothing. She only held on to him, as tightly as she could.

"I never really understood what you'd been through," he said against her hair. "Poor Marilyn Hong—I made her tell me more of the story than she wanted to. She felt like a traitor, but honestly, Hedy, I hadn't known about all the things that had happened to you at Christmas. So then I called Tip and talked to her, too, and got the whole story. I was never fair to you. I was too scared by the emotions you stirred up in me to be fair."

His embrace tightened and pain tinged his voice. "And then you didn't want to see me. I swear part of me died when you were in that hospital. I only felt alive again when you walked back into this house and I took you in my arms."

She hugged him back, but suddenly she went still in his arms. "I—I told Tippy I was coming. She's expecting me."

"No," he said, drawing back and looking into her eyes. "I took a gamble. I told her you weren't coming back. That you were staying."

She wound her arms around Ty's neck. "But Norm came—"

"I flew him down. I didn't think you'd walk out of that hospital with me. He knew all along what we were doing. They both did. I'll fly him back tonight—if you'll stay."

She reached up to push a wayward lock of hair from his forehead. "And Lilka?" she asked gently. "Why did you send her? She's sensational, by the way. She's truly a marvel."

He smiled again. "I sent her because she's sensational and a marvel. And she could tell you all that damnable business about Jolene better than I could. You see, Hedy, you and I really are alike. I don't like talking about the past any more than you do. And I wasn't sure you'd believe me. But nobody ever doubts Lilka—she's just too four-square honest."

Hedy smiled back, although she still felt trembly and misty. "She told me on the way home that you and I are alike. I guess we are."

"Did you hear what you just said?" Ty asked her, locking his hands behind her waist. He kissed her ear, and then her mouth, and then her ear again.

"What?"

"You called this 'home.' Is it?"

She looked at him a long moment. "Yes." Her voice quavered with emotion. "You know it is. Ty..."

"What? I can't look at you enough, Hedy. Why does it make me so idiotically happy just to look at you?"

"About Jolene..." Hedy said, her expression saddening.

His own face went stern. "She's made a lot of trouble. But let's try to forgive and forget. I learned an important lesson from her a long time ago. I lay in that hospital, and I wondered why I'd pushed so hard to succeed. I realized I hated running—I did it for the scholarship. I realized I didn't want to be a lawyer—I was doing it for her. I'd always wanted to write, even if it meant I'd be poor. I realized there was more to life than always being scared you weren't going to make it to the top. I learned that life is short, and you'd better live it. It's a good lesson. And besides, if it wasn't for her, you wouldn't be here, right now, where you belong. Because you belong with me, Hedy. And I belong with you."

"I love you," she said huskily, laying her cheek against his chest again. "And you love me? You really do?"

"Hey," he breathed, bending to kiss her ear. "I've walked ten miles in the snow for you. I've pounded for a week trying to get your furnace installed. You think I'd do that for a woman I just *liked*?"

She smiled and wrinkled her nose at him. "Where's my cat? You've got her, haven't you? I knew a neighbor had her. And it's you, isn't it?"

He shrugged, cocking his head slightly. "Well, yeah. I sent Benchley to Lilka's because he's jealous of the kittens. But Mrs. Parker loves them. She climbs in their box and they play with her ears. So, do you want to get married?"

"What?" She blinked in surprise.

"Married. Get. You and me. I decided in Orlando, but then you slammed the door in my face. But you really ought to marry me. I saved you, you know. And all your cats."

"You even saved the cats?"

"Yes. Don't tell me such heroism goes unrewarded. Take my freedom—please. Marry me."

"Yes," she said, smiling helplessly. "I always wanted to marry into a big family."

"Good. I'll have you know I even had my house painted white again, because I thought you'd like it better."

"I don't care if it's purple," Hedy replied, smoothing his hair back from his brow again. "I don't care if it has hot and cold running ferrets and dogs with hats and pigs with wings. As long as it's on Holly Street and it's with you."

"Everybody's going to want to see you, you know," he said. "It's going to be a little overwhelming. I told them they'd have to wait. I want you to myself for a while. To watch you bloom again."

He folded her closer to him, laid his cheek against her hair. "Hedy," he muttered, his voice roughening with emotion, "we were afraid of losing you—all of us, Marilyn, Peg, Emma—but mostly me. You always reminded me in some crazy way of those decorations I put up every year."

"Decorations?" she asked, nestling against him. "How?"

"Because seeing you open up again is like seeing a garden in the snow." He kissed her ear again. "When I moved here, I asked Lilka to design me something. She's the artistic one. She said, 'I love Chicago, but I hate the winter. I miss the flowers. That's what I'd love to see—flowers in the snow—like a miracle.' So that's what we did. And every year she'd tell me, 'Listen, Ty, you're cynical, but miracles do happen.' She's right. They do. And you're my miracle."

"And you're mine," Hedy replied, "I do love you, Ty. I think I loved you from the moment you walked into the house and reminded me there was still laughter in the world."

His lips hovered over hers. "Merry Christmas, Hedy," he whispered.

"Merry Christmas," she said. "Merry, merry Christmas."

He kissed her.

Outside the old house, the snow covered every yard as far as the eye could see. The prairie afternoon was cloudy, and the Chicago wind keened. But the houses on Holly Street kept blinking their messages: Love. Peace. Comfort. Joy. Hail the New.

And in the brightness of myriad lights, a garden bloomed in the snow.

Coming Next Month

#3025 ARAFURA PIRATE Victoria Gordon
Jinx had been warned about Race Morgan, skipper of the boat taking her scientific research team to Australia's northern coast. But she's confident she can handle it, as long as he keeps their relationship professional.

#3026 GAME PLAN Rosemary Hammond
Jake Donovan, so everyone says, has an infallible plan that makes the women fall at his feet. However, when it doesn't work with reserved Claire Talbot, he finds to his surprise that he can't forget her....

#3027 SPELL OF THE MOUNTAINS Rosalie Henaghan
Sophie is determined to make a success of her motel—and has no intention of selling out to the powerful, dynamic hotelier Jon Roberts. Her refusal only sparks his determination, for Jon isn't used to women who say no!

#3028 JINXED Day Leclaire
Kit soon discovers that playing with toys all day can be a dangerous occupation, especially when working for a man like Stephen "The Iceman" St. Clair. The normally cold and stern owner of The Toy Company behaves more like a volcano whenever Kit is around.

#3029 CONFLICT Margaret Mayo
Blythe's first priority after her father's death is to make the family business pay—and especially to prevent it from falling into Coburn Daggart's hands. Years ago, Coburn hurt her badly, and Blythe makes up her mind to pay him back.

#3030 FOOLISH DECEIVER Sandra K. Rhoades
Allie has learned the hard way that men don't like intelligent women. So, on vacation at an old girlfriend's, she conceals her genius IQ. Her scheme backfires when Linc Summerville believes she is a dumb blonde and treats her like a fool!

Available in January wherever paperback books are sold, or through Harlequin Reader Service:

In the U.S.	In Canada
901 Fuhrmann Blvd.	P.O. Box 603
P.O. Box 1397	Fort Erie, Ontario
Buffalo, N.Y. 14240-1397	L2A 5X3

INDULGE A LITTLE SWEEPSTAKES

OFFICIAL RULES

SWEEPSTAKES RULES AND REGULATIONS. NO PURCHASE NECESSARY.

1. NO PURCHASE NECESSARY. To enter complete the official entry form and return with the invoice in the envelope provided. Or you may enter by printing your name, complete address and your daytime phone number on a 3 x 5 piece of paper. Include with your entry the hand printed words "Indulge A Little Sweepstakes." Mail your entry to: Indulge A Little Sweepstakes, P.O. Box 1397, Buffalo, NY 14269-1397. No mechanically reproduced entries accepted. Not responsible for late, lost, misdirected mail, or printing errors.

2. Three winners, one per month (Sept. 30, 1989, October 31, 1989 and November 30, 1989), will be selected in random drawings. All entries received prior to the drawing date will be eligible for that month's prize. This sweepstakes is under the supervision of MARDEN-KANE, INC. an independent judging organization whose decisions are final and binding. Winners will be notified by telephone and may be required to execute an affidavit of eligibility and release which must be returned within 14 days, or an alternate winner will be selected.

3. Prizes: 1st Grand Prize (1) a trip for two to Disneyworld in Orlando, Florida. Trip includes round trip air transportation, hotel accommodations for seven days and six nights, plus up to $700 expense money (ARV $3,500). 2nd Grand Prize (1) a seven-night Chandris Caribbean Cruise for two includes transportation from nearest major airport, accommodations, meals plus up to $1,000 in expense money (ARV $4,300). 3rd Grand Prize (1) a ten day Hawaiian holiday for two includes round trip air transportation for two, hotel accommodations, sightseeing, plus up to $1,200 in spending money (ARV $7,700). All trips subject to availability and must be taken as outlined on the entry form.

4. Sweepstakes open to residents of the U.S. and Canada 18 years or older except employees and the families of Torstar Corp., its affiliates, subsidiaries and Marden-Kane, Inc. and all other agencies and persons connected with conducting this sweepstakes. All Federal, State and local laws and regulations apply. Void wherever prohibited or restricted by law. Taxes, if any are the sole responsibility of the prize winners. Canadian winners will be required to answer a skill testing question. Winners consent to the use of their name, photograph and/or likeness for publicity purposes without additional compensation.

5. For a list of prize winners, send a stamped, self-addressed envelope to Indulge A Little Sweepstakes Winners, P.O. Box 701, Sayreville, NJ 08871.

DL-SWPS

INDULGE A LITTLE SWEEPSTAKES

OFFICIAL RULES

SWEEPSTAKES RULES AND REGULATIONS. NO PURCHASE NECESSARY.

1. NO PURCHASE NECESSARY. To enter complete the official entry form and return with the invoice in the envelope provided. Or you may enter by printing your name, complete address and your daytime phone number on a 3 x 5 piece of paper. Include with your entry the hand printed words "Indulge A Little Sweepstakes." Mail your entry to: Indulge A Little Sweepstakes, P.O. Box 1397, Buffalo, NY 14269-1397. No mechanically reproduced entries accepted. Not responsible for late, lost, misdirected mail, or printing errors.

2. Three winners, one per month (Sept. 30, 1989, October 31, 1989 and November 30, 1989), will be selected in random drawings. All entries received prior to the drawing date will be eligible for that month's prize. This sweepstakes is under the supervision of MARDEN-KANE, INC. an independent judging organization whose decisions are final and binding. Winners will be notified by telephone and may be required to execute an affidavit of eligibility and release which must be returned within 14 days, or an alternate winner will be selected.

3. Prizes: 1st Grand Prize (1) a trip for two to Disneyworld in Orlando, Florida. Trip includes round trip air transportation, hotel accommodations for seven days and six nights, plus up to $700 expense money (ARV $3,500). 2nd Grand Prize (1) a seven-night Chandris Caribbean Cruise for two includes transportation from nearest major airport, accommodations, meals plus up to $1,000 in expense money (ARV $4,300). 3rd Grand Prize (1) a ten-day Hawaiian holiday for two includes round trip air transportation for two, hotel accommodations, sightseeing, plus up to $1,200 in spending money (ARV $7,700). All trips subject to availability and must be taken as outlined on the entry form.

4. Sweepstakes open to residents of the U.S. and Canada 18 years or older except employees and the families of Torstar Corp., its affiliates, subsidiaries and Marden-Kane, Inc. and all other agencies and persons connected with conducting this sweepstakes. All Federal, State and local laws and regulations apply. Void wherever prohibited or restricted by law. Taxes, if any are the sole responsibility of the prize winners. Canadian winners will be required to answer a skill testing question. Winners consent to the use of their name, photograph and/or likeness for publicity purposes without additional compensation.

5. For a list of prize winners, send a stamped, self-addressed envelope to Indulge A Little Sweepstakes Winners, P.O. Box 701, Sayreville, NJ 08871.

© 1989 HARLEQUIN ENTERPRISES LTD.

DL-SWPS

INDULGE A LITTLE—WIN A LOT!

Summer of '89 Subscribers-Only Sweepstakes

OFFICIAL ENTRY FORM

This entry must be received by: Nov. 30, 1989
This month's winner will be notified by: Dec. 7, 1989
Trip must be taken between: Jan. 7, 1990–Jan. 7, 1991

YES, I want to win the 3-Island Hawaiian vacation for two! I understand the prize includes round-trip airfare, first-class hotels, and a daily allowance as revealed on the "Wallet" scratch-off card.

Name____________________

Address____________________

City________ State/Prov.______ Zip/Postal Code______

Daytime phone number________________
Area code

Return entries with invoice in envelope provided. Each book in this shipment has two entry coupons — and the more coupons you enter, the better your chances of winning!

DINDL-3

INDULGE A LITTLE—WIN A LOT!

Summer of '89 Subscribers-Only Sweepstakes

OFFICIAL ENTRY FORM

This entry must be received by: Nov. 30, 1989
This month's winner will be notified by: Dec. 7, 1989
Trip must be taken between: Jan. 7, 1990–Jan. 7, 1991

YES, I want to win the 3-Island Hawaiian vacation for two! I understand the prize includes round-trip airfare, first-class hotels, and a daily allowance as revealed on the "Wallet" scratch-off card.

Name____________________

Address____________________

City________ State/Prov.______ Zip/Postal Code______

Daytime phone number________________
Area code

Return entries with invoice in envelope provided. Each book in this shipment has two entry coupons — and the more coupons you enter, the better your chances of winning!

© 1989 HARLEQUIN ENTERPRISES LTD.

DINDL-3